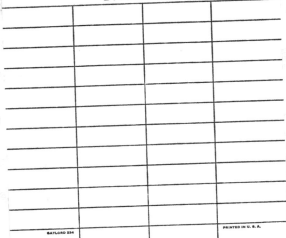

DATE DUE

GAYLORD 234   PRINTED IN U. S. A.

DISCARDED

Me and
My Little Brain

by John D. Fitzgerald

ILLUSTRATED BY MERCER MAYER

A YEARLING BOOK

Published by
Dell Publishing
a division of
Bantam Doubleday Dell Publishing Group, Inc.
1540 Broadway
New York, New York 10036

For Angela and Raymond

ISBN: 0-440-45533-2

Reprinted by arrangement with Dial Books for Young Readers, a division of
Penguin USA Inc.

Printed in the United States of America

One Previous Edition

March 1988

31   30   29   28   27   26

OPM

Contents

CHAPTER 1
The Wheeler-Dealer 3

CHAPTER 2
A Born Loser 18

CHAPTER 3
Frankie Pennyworth 38

CHAPTER 4
Curing Frankie's Mental Block 54

CHAPTER 5
Frankie Takes Over 69

CHAPTER 6
The Escape of Cal Roberts   90

CHAPTER 7
Hostage   106

CHAPTER 8
My Little Brain Against Cal Roberts   121

CHAPTER ONE

The Wheeler-Dealer

ON THE SECOND MONDAY of September in 1897
I was sitting on top of the world. Well, to tell the truth, I
wasn't actually sitting on top of the world. I just felt as if I
were. I was sitting on the top rail of our corral fence watching Frank Jensen doing all my chores. It reminded me of the
hundreds of times my brother Tom had sat on the corral
fence watching me do all his chores. He had bamboozled me
into doing his share of the work so many times that Mamma
and Aunt Bertha were both astonished whenever they saw
him carrying in a bucketful of coal or an armful of kindling
wood. And that is why I felt as if I were sitting on top of the
world.

I had been the victim of Tom's great brain more times than a horse switches its tail knocking off flies in the summertime. He had swindled me out of my birthday and Christmas presents until there was no sense in me having a birthday or receiving Christmas presents. I wasn't the only kid in Adenville, Utah, who had been victimized by my brother's great brain. Tom didn't play any favorites when it came to being the youngest confidence man who ever lived. There wasn't a kid in town who hadn't been swindled by my brother.

I didn't hold a grudge against Tom for the many times he had put one over on me. I was actually grateful. When a fellow has been the victim of every confidence trick in the book, he gets to be pretty darn sharp himself. So sharp, I was positive I could step right into Tom's shoes after he left for the Catholic Academy in Salt Lake City with my oldest brother, Sweyn.

Adenville had a population of about two thousand Mormons and about five hundred Protestants and Catholics. We had a one-room schoolhouse where Mr. Standish taught the first through the sixth grades. Any parents who wanted their children to get a higher education had to send them to Salt Lake City. Sweyn was starting his second year at the Academy. Tom was only eleven but going to the Academy because he was so smart Mr. Standish had let him skip a grade. I was only nine years old and wouldn't be going away to school for a few years.

I thought I would bawl like a baby when Tom left. I felt sad about having a brother I loved leave home. I knew I would miss him very much. But at the same time I couldn't help feeling sort of relieved.

Mamma and Aunt Bertha carried on as if my brothers were going off to war as the train left the depot.

"I feel so sorry for my two boys," Mamma cried. "They are so very young to be leaving home."

Papa put his arm around Mamma's shoulders. "If you must feel sorry for anybody," he said, "feel sorry for the Jesuit priests at the Academy who are going to have to put up with the Great Brain for the next nine months."

I know that sounds like a cruel thing for a father to say. Papa was editor and publisher of the *Adenville Weekly Advocate* and was considered one of the smartest men in town. But Tom had made a fool out of Papa almost as many times as he had me. Maybe that was why Papa had said what he did. Sometimes I thought Tom had made Papa and me his favorite victims because we looked so much alike. I was a real leaf off the Fitzgerald family tree. I had the same dark curly hair and deep brown eyes that Papa had. Anybody could tell I just had to be his son by looking at us. Sweyn was a blond and looked like our Danish mother. Tom didn't look like Papa and he didn't look like Mamma unless you sort of put them both together.

I couldn't help feeling a sense of great power after Tom was gone from Adenville. I knew I only had a little brain compared with Tom's great brain. But I believed I'd learned enough from my brother to outsmart any kid in town. I knew I wasn't a genius like Tom when it came to putting one over on Papa or Mamma and other adults in town. But my brother had taught me that adults are pretty dumb, and a kid who uses his head can fool them most of the time. The time had come for me to take over where Tom had left off.

Tom and I had each received ten cents a week allowance

for doing our chores. I know that doesn't sound like much, but back in the 1890's a dime would buy what it costs fifty cents or more to buy today. Soda pop was only a penny and so was a double-scoop ice cream cone. Papa increased my allowance to twenty cents a week for doing all the chores after Tom left home. This was a windfall because Tom had connived me into doing all the chores about ninety percent of the time anyway. I could see no reason for me ever doing any more chores now that I had an allowance of twenty cents a week.

I didn't get a chance to start wheeling and dealing until the Saturday after school started. I rode Tom's bike over to where Frank and Allan Jensen lived, on the outskirts of town. I knew the Jensen family was very poor. Allan was fourteen but his parents couldn't afford to send him away to school. Frank was twelve years old. They both had blond hair that was almost white. It grew funny down over their foreheads so a shock of it was always sticking out under the visors of their caps.

They were hauling manure from their barn to spread on their big vegetable garden. Everybody put manure on their gardens in the fall. Then in the spring they would spade or plow it under before planting. It not only fertilized the ground but also kept all kinds of bugs out of the gardens.

Frank and Allan were using a stone sled to haul the manure. Practically everybody owned a stone sled in those days. They were made with two-by-four runners sawed at an angle in front. More two-by-fours or thick boards were used to build a platform. Holes were drilled in the front part of the runners. A rope or chain was hooked through the holes and to the tugs of a horse's harness. They were called stone sleds because they were originally used by early pioneers to

6

haul stones to build fireplaces. They were very handy for small hauling jobs instead of using a wagon. Frank and Allan were in their barn loading manure on their stone sled with pitchforks when I walked in, wheeling Tom's bike.

"I have a proposition to make you," I said.

They both stopped working and leaned on the handles of their pitchforks.

Allan asked, "What kind of a proposition?"

"I'll pay you five cents a week to do my chores," I said. "You can take turns each week."

Allan looked steadily at me. "Just what do you call chores?" he asked.

"Once a day you fill up all the woodboxes and coal buckets in the parlor, dining room, bathroom, and kitchen," I said. "And you feed and water our team of horses and the milk cow and Sweyn's mustang, Dusty. And you milk the cow and feed and water the chickens."

Allan shook his head. "That is a lot of work for just a nickel a week," he said.

I was expecting him to say just that. Tom had taught me when making a deal to always offer only half at first. Then when you double it, a kid will think he is getting a good deal.

"I'll make it a dime a week," I said. "That will give each of you a nickel a week spending money."

Allan looked at his brother and then back at me. "No mowing the lawn or weeding the garden or chopping kindling wood or things like that?" he asked.

"No," I said. "If the lawn needs cutting or there are weeds to pull, I'll do it. And my father always chops our kindling wood for exercise."

Allan nodded. "We'll take it," he said. "When do we start?"

7

"Monday after school," I answered.

"When do we get paid?" Allan asked.

"I'll pay you every Monday for the previous week's work," I said.

We all shook hands to seal the bargain. I'd pulled off my first big deal. Frank and Allan would be doing all my chores for ten cents a week. That left me a neat profit of a dime a week for doing nothing. Now all I had to do was think up a good story to tell Papa and Mamma.

I couldn't help feeling very proud of myself as I rode Tom's bike down Main Street on my way home. I had Adenville in the palm of my hand. It wouldn't surprise me if I ended up becoming the youngest mayor in Utah. As its mayor, Adenville was a town of which I could be proud. It was a typical Utah town, depending upon agriculture since the closing of the mines in the nearby ghost town of Silverlode. We had electric lights and telephones. The streets were wide and covered with gravel. There were wooden sidewalks in front of the stores. We had sidewalks made from ashes and cinders in front of homes. All the streets were lined with trees planted by early Mormon pioneers. The railroad tracks separated the west side of town from the east side. All the homes and most of the places of business were on the west side. There were just a couple of saloons, the Sheepmen's Hotel, Palace Cafe, the livery stable, the blacksmith shop, and a couple of other stores and a rooming house on the east side.

When I rode down an alley and into our backyard, my dog Brownie and his pup Prince came running to meet me. I put the bike on the back porch after patting them on the heads. Brownie was a thoroughbred Alaskan malamute. The pup was the pick of the litter after I'd mated Brownie with a sheep dog named Lady owned by Frank and Allan Jensen.

I walked to our barn and climbed up the rope ladder to the loft. Papa and Mr. Jamison, the carpenter, had built the loft for me and my brothers. They had laid boards across three beam rafters and nailed them down. They had also made a wooden ladder up the side of the barn to the loft. Tom, in his usual style, had taken possession of the loft. He had removed the wooden ladder and replaced it with a rope ladder. This way he could climb into the loft and pull the rope ladder up after him so nobody else could come up.

Tom had an accumulation of stuff in the loft ranging from an old trunk of Mamma's to the skull of an Indian that Uncle Mark had given him. My Uncle Mark was the Marshal of Adenville and a Deputy Sheriff. Adenville was the county seat and my uncle was Acting Sheriff most of the time. Sheriff Baker spent a great deal of time tracking down Paiute Indians who left the reservation in the county, and renegade Navaho Indians who made raids into Southwestern Utah from Arizona. People said that Sheriff Baker took care of the Indians and Uncle Mark took care of white lawbreakers.

I sat down on one of the boxes in the loft. I put my right hand under my chin and my elbow on my right knee just like a picture I'd seen of a statue called "The Thinker." I figured this position would help me think up a good story to tell Papa and Mamma. But I found out the sculptor who had made the statue didn't know beans about thinking. I couldn't think because the position was so darn uncomfortable. I lay down on my back and stared up at the roof instead. I knew if I told Papa and Mamma I'd hired Frank and Allan to do my chores for ten cents a week what they would say. They would say if I was going to hire somebody to do my chores I should pay them the whole twenty cents a week.

When I went to bed that night I still hadn't thought up

a good story. Then I remembered something Tom had told me one time. He had said that a person's subconscious mind was a hundred times smarter than his conscious mind. And he'd told me that if a person just thinks about a problem before going to sleep, the subconscious mind would solve the problem while the person was asleep. And when you woke up in the morning the answer would be in your conscious mind. It sounded complicated to me. But I was really concentrating on what I'd tell Papa and Mamma when I fell asleep that night.

And, by jingo, it worked! When I woke up in the morning I had my story. I waited until after supper that Sunday evening to tell it. Papa was sitting in his rocking chair reading the mail edition of the New York *World*. Mamma was sitting in her maple rocker crocheting. The light from the ceiling chandelier made her blonde hair, piled high with braids on her head, shine as if it were golden. Aunt Bertha was sitting on the couch darning some socks. She wasn't really my aunt. She had come to live with us after her husband died. She was sixty years old and had hands and feet as big as a man's. I was sitting on the Oriental rug in front of our huge stone fireplace.

"I was talking to Frank and Allan Jensen yesterday," I said. "I sure feel sorry for them."

Papa dropped the newspaper on his lap. "What makes you say that, J.D.?" he asked. Papa always called us boys by our initials.

"Because they are so poor," I said, "the only time they ever get a piece of candy is at Christmas time."

"Mr. Jensen is a poor but proud man," Papa said. "But I do know the family has enough to eat because the Mormons never let another Mormon go hungry."

"But don't you think every boy is entitled to some candy more than just once a year?" I asked.

"Yes, I do," Papa answered.

I knew I had him. I'd made Papa walk right into my trap. Now all I needed was to make Mamma second the motion.

"How about you, Mamma?" I asked.

"Candy is a part of boyhood," she said. "I must remember the next time I make some candy to send some over to Mrs. Jensen."

"You won't have to," I said. "I fixed it so Frank and Allan can have some candy every week."

Papa stared at me. "And just how did you arrange that?" he asked.

"I'm going to pay them ten cents a week out of my allowance to help me do my chores," I said. "Frank will help one week and Allan the next week. That will give each of them a nickel spending money every week."

"I'm proud of you, son," Papa said, and I knew when he called me "son" he was feeling very proud of me.

"God bless you," Mamma said.

"Amen," Aunt Bertha said.

I was so excited I felt like doing an Indian war dance right in our parlor. I'd begun my career as a wheeler-dealer by pulling off my first big deal.

And that is how come I was sitting on the top rail of our corral fence the next day after school feeling as if I were sitting on top of the world. But I sure as heck wasn't sitting there very long.

Mamma kept looking at me in a funny sort of way all through our roast pork supper with homemade gooseberry

pie for dessert. She didn't say anything until we'd finished eating and she had folded her napkin and put it in the silver napkin ring.

"I thought, John D.," she said, "that Frank and Allan were just supposed to help you with your chores. From what I saw this first day it appeared that Frank did all your chores. And all you did was sit on the corral fence watching him."

I had to think fast. The answer came so quickly that I began to believe I had a great brain like Tom.

"Frank and Allan appreciate what I'm doing for them so much," I said, "that they insisted on doing all my chores."

"Good," Mamma said, to my surprise.

Papa was also surprised. "What is good about it?" he asked. "It seems to me we got rid of one conniver by sending him off to Salt Lake City only to discover we have another one in our midst."

Mamma smiled. "Don't you see, dear, this means John D. will have time to do other things that need to be done."

I didn't like the sound of it. "What other things?" I asked.

"You can begin tomorrow after school by spreading manure on our vegetable garden," Mamma said.

That was when I learned something about mothers I didn't know. They just couldn't stand to see their sons taking it easy. I looked at Papa with pleading eyes. He had always said it was brains that counted and not muscle. He would appreciate how smart I had been. I couldn't have been more wrong than a mouse who spits in a cat's face.

"That is a splendid idea," Papa said, as if he enjoyed making a slave out of his own flesh and blood. "I thought I might have to hire a man to do it, with Tom gone. But J.D. is big enough to handle it."

"And when he finishes that job," Mamma said, as if she were doing me a big favor, "he can help Bertha and me with the fall housecleaning. The wallpaper needs cleaning in all the upstairs rooms and in the two bedrooms downstairs. He won't have to bother with the parlor and dining room because I'm going to put new wallpaper in both rooms. And there will be windows to wash and rugs to beat and a lot of other things he can do to help."

I knew there was no appealing one of Mamma's decisions. I also knew that if I listened to any more I'd burst out crying. I excused myself from the table and ran up to my room. I threw myself on the bed. I tried to hold back the tears but couldn't. If ever a fellow had a right to cry, I sure did.

I would ten times rather do my chores than haul manure, which meant I had to take a bath every night before supper. I would a hundred times rather do my chores than help with the fall housecleaning. And the worst part of housecleaning was cleaning the wallpaper. You had to do it with a homemade dough that really smelled bad. I don't know what Mamma put into it but it was like having a skunk in your hand. And you had to rub it over every inch of the wallpaper. I admit it really cleaned wallpaper, taking off the grime and dirt just like an eraser. But it was back-breaking work and the smell was enough to make a fellow sick to his stomach.

For the next four days after school and all day on Saturday I hauled manure and took baths. Papa had often said that a man profits more spiritually from failure than he does from success. But I sure as heck didn't get any spiritual uplift unless maybe taking so many baths washed some of my sins away.

But I wasn't going to let one failure get me down. I'd made the best deal of my life with Tom by renting his bike from him for ten cents a week while he was away at school. I had a scheme all figured out for making a fortune with the bike. Monday morning during recess I got all the kids together who didn't own bikes. I told them I would rent out Tom's bike for five cents a day and would be in our barn to sign up customers after school.

I stopped at the Z.C.M.I. store after school and got a calendar from Mr. Harmon. The full name was Zion's Cooperative Mercantile Institute. They were stores owned by the Church of Jesus Christ of Latter-day Saints all over Utah which sold everything from toothpicks to wagons.

Sammy Leeds was waiting in our barn when I arrived. He was puffing as if he'd run all the way from the schoolhouse. I didn't like Sammy because he was a smart aleck and bully, but business was business. I was both surprised and delighted when Sammy said he would take twenty days and dumped a total of one dollar in dimes, nickels, and pennies in a box I had in the barn.

I tore off all the months on the calendar up to September and told Sammy to write his name on the twenty days he wanted to rent the bike. Parley Benson, wearing his coonskin cap, came into the barn with Basil Kokovinis, a Greek boy whose father owned the Palace Cafe. Danny Forester, Howard Kay, Jimmie Peterson, and Seth Smith came in right behind them. They waited until Sammy had signed his name twenty times on the calendar and I had marked each day paid.

"Before you fellows lay your money on the line," Sammy said, "I've taken all the Saturdays and Sundays for the next ten weeks. That means I'll get to ride the bike all day for

15

my nickel but you fellows will only get to ride it after school for a couple of hours for your nickel."

Parley pushed his coonskin cap to the back of his head. "I sure ain't going to pay to rent a bike when I'm sitting in school," he said.

He and the other kids looked at me as if I'd just tried to rob their piggy banks, and walked out of the barn.

"Tell you what I'll do," Sammy said. "Seeing as how I would only get to use the bike for a couple of hours on school days, I'll give you a penny a day. I know the other kids would pay you a penny too, but there will be days when nobody will rent the bike. I'll pay you cash right now for the next fifty school days."

I knew Sammy was right, and five-cents-a-week profit was better than taking a chance of not renting the bike on some school days.

"Why do you want the bike all for yourself for ten weeks?" I asked.

"Mr. Nicholson at the drugstore wants a delivery boy with a bike to work after school and on Saturdays," Sammy said. "You will be helping me get the job, John, and you know my folks are poor and we can use the money."

"The drugstore is closed on Sundays," I said. "Why did you want Sundays too?"

"A fellow is entitled to a little fun after working all week, ain't he?" Sammy asked.

I sure as heck didn't want to be known as a fellow who stopped a boy from getting a job and helping out his folks.

"It's a deal," I said.

Sammy put his hand in another pocket and took out exactly fifty cents in change as if he had known what was going to happen.

The next day after school I had to deliver the weekly edition of Papa's newspaper to local subscribers at their homes and the ones with yellow mail stickers on them to the post office. Papa saw I was using my wagon instead of Tom's bike. I told him about the deal that I had made with Sammy Leeds. Papa pushed his green eyeshade up on his forehead.

"I'm glad you helped Sammy get a job," he said, "but you had no right renting out something you do not own. And I hope you realize Sammy will just about wear out the tires in ten weeks on these gravel streets."

"That is Tom's tough luck," I said.

"No, J.D., that is your tough luck," Papa said. "You will buy new tires for your brother's bicycle."

"But they will cost about three dollars," I protested, "and I am only making fifty cents on the whole deal."

"I am sure you have enough money in your bank to buy the new tires when the time comes," Papa said.

If I thought that was bad, the worst was yet to come. Sammy let all the kids know that Mr. Nicholson was paying him two dollars a week and in ten weeks he would have more than enough money saved to buy a bike of his own. He also told all the kids he would be at Smith's vacant lot on Sundays and they could rent the bike for a penny an hour.

I learned later that Sammy had made seven cents renting the bike for one-hour rides that first Sunday. I knew he would go on making money every Sunday. And, oh, how I wished my little brain had thought of the idea first. Boy, oh, boy, what a catastrophe my career as a wheeler-dealer had turned out to be. If Papa was right about a fellow profiting spiritually from failure, I'd soon become the holiest kid in the world at the rate I was going.

CHAPTER TWO

A Born Loser

MAMMA AND AUNT BERTHA had towels tied around their heads when Papa and I entered the kitchen for breakfast the next morning. It was their way of notifying us that fall housecleaning was to begin that day. During the next six days I discovered that Abraham Lincoln left out something when he freed the slaves—he forgot to include *kids* in the Emancipation Proclamation. I was so plumb tuckered out at night I could hardly do my homework. We finished all the housecleaning on Saturday. That was one Saturday night when Mamma didn't have to remind me it was time for my bath.

"I am going to take my bath and go to bed," I said as

we all sat in the parlor after supper was over.

Mamma looked at the clock on the mantlepiece. "At seven o'clock?" she asked.

"Not only that," I said, "but please don't call me until it is time to get up to go to school on Monday."

Mamma smiled at me. "You have worked very hard, John D.," she said. "And when a person does his best without thought of reward it proves he has a good character."

I had my own ideas about character but didn't mention them. There is something about housecleaning that completely changes a woman's character. Mamma had been a strange woman with a very sharp tongue for six days. She had been bossing me around all that time. I felt like telling her that us slaves didn't care whether we had a good or a bad character. But I was just too tired to start an argument.

"Good night," I said.

"Just a minute," Mamma said. "Your father has something for you."

I forgot how tired I was as I watched Papa take out his purse and remove a half-dollar from it.

"Your mother tells me you have earned this, J.D.," he said.

"Thanks, Papa, and you too, Mamma," I said, as astonished as I was grateful. I was astonished at how dumb I'd been in thinking Papa and Mamma thought of me as just a free hired hand around the place. I was grateful because a half-dollar was a fortune.

Papa celebrated the end of the fall housecleaning by inviting a stranger to dinner the next day. Papa was always inviting strangers to Sunday dinner. I mean, they were strangers to Mamma, Aunt Bertha, and me. Papa knew all the traveling salesmen who came to town. They were called "drummers" in those days. He also knew people who lived on ranches miles from town who only came to Adenville a couple of times each year. He made it his business to meet every stranger who arrived, From all these people he got news about other parts of Utah which he published in his newspaper. But Papa had a bad habit of always forgetting to tell Mamma he had invited somebody for Sunday dinner. She was used to it and always made sure there was plenty to eat for these unexpected guests.

It was no surprise to Mamma when she answered the front doorbell at noon and saw a complete stranger standing before her. He was a tall middle-aged man with a black mustache so long it wiggled when he talked.

"You must be Mrs. Fitzgerald," he said, taking off his black hat. "Permit me to introduce myself. I am Alex Kramer. Your husband invited me for Sunday dinner."

"Come right in, Mr. Kramer," Mamma said. "My husband will be with you in a few minutes. There are cigars in the humidor if you care to smoke. Dinner will be ready in about half an hour."

"Thank you kindly, ma'am," Mr. Kramer said.

Papa was on the back porch with me. We were repacking the ice cream freezer with ice and salt. We had made the ice cream earlier. We had to be careful because we both had on our Sunday clothes. We had just finished when Mamma came to the back porch.

"Just who is Alex Kramer?" she asked.

Papa snapped his fingers. "I forgot to tell you, Tena," he said. "I invited Alex to dinner."

"You didn't answer my question," Mamma said.

Papa hesitated for a moment. "Well, you might say that Alex is a trader," he said.

"And what else might you say about him?" Mamma asked.

Papa shrugged. "I suppose some people would call him a sharpie," he said. "And others might go so far as to call him a swindler of sorts."

"I knew it just by looking at him," Mamma said, as if exasperated. "You just don't seem to care who you invite into our home, do you?"

"Alex is all right," Papa said. "I trust him implicitly. And he is a very interesting man to talk to."

"Just make certain you count the cigars in your humidor when you go into the parlor," Mamma said. "Bertha and I will count the silverware after dinner."

Papa stared at the screen door as Mamma slammed it going into the kitchen. "It is a strange thing about women, J.D.," he said, shaking his head. "A man never knows what to expect from them. And the longer you are married to them, the less you know what to expect. We will wash our hands and then I'll introduce you to Mr. Kramer."

The man in the parlor was wearing a blue suit and shiny black boots. He had on a ruffled shirt with a shoestring necktie. He was smoking a cigar. And I couldn't help noticing that he had five cigars in the breast pocket of his suit. Papa noticed too.

"I see you found the cigars, Alex," he said.

"Didn't think you would mind, Fitz," Mr. Kramer said. Hardly anybody called Papa by his first name. Men, especially, called him Fitz.

"Meet my youngest son, John," Papa said. "John, this is Mr. Kramer."

Mr. Kramer shook my hand. "Glad to know you, young man," he said.

21

"I'm glad to know you, sir," I said.

Mr. Kramer looked at Papa. "Your wife is both beautiful and charming," he said.

I wondered how charming he would have thought Mamma was if he could have heard what she said about him.

"Thank you," Papa said. "Sit down, Alex. We have time for a smoke before dinner."

Mr. Kramer sat down on the black leather chair that matched our couch. Papa sat in his rocking chair. He took a cigar from the humidor and used the clipper on the end of his watch chain to snip off the end. Then he lit the cigar and leaned back in his chair.

"It has been a long time, Alex," Papa said, blowing some smoke toward the ceiling. "The last time I saw you I was publishing the *Silverlode Advocate* before the mining camp became a ghost town."

"Must be close to fifteen years," Mr. Kramer said.

"How is business with you?" Papa asked.

"Not too good," Mr. Kramer answered. "I remember the time when I could start out with a sheep dog and trade myself right up to a good team of horses in no time at all. Either I am getting rusty or people are getting smarter."

Papa laughed as he exhaled some smoke. "I remember one time in Silverlode when you started out with a pocketknife and ended up with a milk cow."

"I recall that deal," Mr. Kramer said, puffing on his cigar. "I bought the pocketknife in Abie Glassman's Emporium for fifty cents. I sold the milk cow to a Mormon for twenty dollars."

"I think you topped that one the time you started out with a burro and ended up with a team of horses and a buggy," Papa said.

I was listening so hard it felt as if my ears had doubled in size. Mr. Kramer made my brother Tom look like a piker. I knew it was rude to interrupt my elders but I was so curious I couldn't help it.

"How did you do those things, Mr. Kramer?" I asked. He looked at Papa before answering.

"Go ahead," Papa said. "It might save J.D. from getting skinned trading some time."

Mr. Kramer knocked the ashes on his cigar into the ashtray. "It is what you might call trading up," he said. "First you find somebody who wants something they don't have more than they want something they own. You always get the best of the bargain because they are eager to exchange something they don't particularly need for something they really do want. Let us assume that you are a prospector and you own a horse but would rather have a burro. So you trade the horse for a burro although you know the horse is worth more."

"Thank you for explaining," I said. I just couldn't understand why Papa had called Mr. Kramer a sharpie. For my money he was just doing people a favor, getting them something they wanted for something they didn't want.

"I came into town riding a gentle saddle horse," Mr. Kramer said to Papa. "It would make a good horse for a lady. Know anybody who needs one?"

"Not offhand," Papa said. "But if you can get your hands on a good team of mules I know where you can get a very good price for them. Pete Ferguson, who runs a logging camp about twenty miles from here, is looking for a good team of mules."

Mr. Kramer smiled. "Then I'll just have to trade my saddle horse up to a team of mules," he said.

"And I will bet you do it," Papa said with a laugh. Then his face became serious. "How are you fixed for money, Alex?"

"I was hoping you would ask," Mr. Kramer said. "I could use the loan of twenty dollars until I get Mr. Ferguson his team of mules."

Papa took out his purse. He handed Mr. Kramer four five-dollar gold pieces. Then he looked at me.

"Mum's the word, J.D.," he said.

"Mum's the word," I said, knowing Mamma wouldn't like Papa handing out twenty dollars to a man she believed to be a swindler. And I couldn't help wondering what made Papa think he could trust Mr. Kramer to pay him back.

In a little while Mamma came into the parlor with Aunt Bertha. She introduced Aunt Bertha to Mr. Kramer and then said that dinner was ready.

Papa was sure right about Mr. Kramer being an interesting man. He had Mamma and Aunt Bertha eating right out of his hand as he told them about the latest in ladies' fashions, and about some plays he'd seen at the Salt Lake Theater his last trip there. But best of all were the stories he told Papa and me later in the parlor while Mamma and Aunt Bertha were doing the dishes. One of them I remember very well.

There was an old prospector named Harvey Reynolds who had been prospecting all over Colorado, Utah, and Nevada for many years without ever making a strike. He had a claim he was working near Eureka, Utah. One day he walked over to where another prospector named Gordon was working a claim. He offered to trade his claim to Gordon for six sticks of dynamite. The trade was made and Reynolds signed his claim over to Gordon. Then Reynolds said he wanted to get some tools out of the shaft of his claim. Instead, he went down to the bottom of the shaft, sat down on the six sticks of dynamite, and touched them off, blowing himself to smithereens. Gordon heard the explosion and ran over to the claim. He had to wait until the dust from the explosion had settled. There wasn't much left of Reynolds when Gordon got to the bottom of the shaft. But the dynamite blast had uncovered one of the richest veins of gold ore ever discovered in Eureka. Harvey Reynolds was within a foot of hitting this vein when he blew himself to kingdom come.

The next morning I took a notebook with me to school. Mr. Alex Kramer had given me an idea which would make me the richest kid in Adenville and maybe in all of Utah. I figured if an adult could trade up, so could a kid. During the morning and afternoon recesses I talked to nine kids. When I came home from school I had the following list:

Howard Kay Wants an Indian Suit and War Bonnet
Jimmie Peterson Wants a Cap Pistol and Holster
Roger Gillis Wants a Wagon
Basil Kokovinis Wants an Air Rifle
Parley Benson Wants a Belgian Hare Doe Rabbit
Frank Jensen Wants an Indian Scout Knife
Seth Smith Wants a Genuine Indian Bow and Arrow
Danny Forester Wants a Riding Quirt
Andy Anderson Wants a Male Puppy

I went up to my room to study the list. Mr. Kramer had said all a trader had to do was to find something somebody wanted. I knew what all these kids wanted. But I didn't know what they had that they didn't particularly want or need. Then, as I studied the list, I saw how easy it was going to be.

I figured I'd start my trading with Howard Kay. My brother Tom's Indian suit and war bonnet were too small for him but would just fit Howard. Mamma was a saver who never threw anything away. She had just about everything Sweyn, Tom, and I had ever worn stored in the attic. I went up to the attic. It took some rummaging around, but I finally found the Indian suit and war bonnet stored in a box with old cowboy suits and other things.

Howard was sitting on the steps of his back porch when I arrived.

"Would you rather have an Indian suit and war bonnet or your cap pistol and holster?" I asked him.

He looked at me with a puzzled expression on his pumpkin-like face. "Why do you want another cap pistol?" he asked.

"I'm just doing you a favor because you're my friend," I said. "You told me this morning you wanted an Indian suit and war bonnet."

"I do," he said. "And I'll tell you why. When we play cowboy and Indians or cavalry and Indians I never get to be one of the tricky Indians. I've always wanted to be a tricky Indian but couldn't because I didn't have an Indian suit and war bonnet. I'll trade you, John. I only get to use the cap pistol on the fourth of July anyway. That is the only time my folks will let me buy caps for it."

I left Howard's home with the cap pistol and holster. My next stop was the boardinghouse that Jimmie Peterson's mother owned. Poor Jimmie had to peel potatoes for the boarders almost every day after school. I found him on his back porch peeling spuds and dropping them into a bucket of water. I showed him the cap pistol and holster.

"How would you like to own it?" I asked.

He stood up and wiped his hands on the front of his shirt. Then he put on the holster and made a couple of practice draws with the cap pistol.

"What do you want for it?" he asked.

"I remember you telling me one of your mother's boarders gave you a scout knife for Christmas last year," I said. "That means you've got two scout knives. I'll trade you the cap pistol and holster for one of them.

Jimmie thought for a moment. "A scout knife is worth more than a cap pistol and holster," he said.

"Just tell me how you can whittle or do anything with two scout knives at the same time," I said. "It's like having four legs when you only need two to walk on. I figured I was doing you a favor by taking one of the knives off your hands and trading you something you really need and want."

I knew I had him when Jimmie made a couple more practice draws.

"I'll trade my old scout knife but not the new one," he said.

"It's a deal," I said.

I left Jimmie's back porch feeling mighty proud of myself as a trader. I'd started out with Tom's old Indian suit and war bonnet that was just lying around in our attic and now had a scout knife.

The next day after school I told Frank Jensen I wanted to talk to him. It was his brother Allan's week to do my chores. I knew their dog Lady had given birth to another litter of pups, which were now weaned. Some mongrel dog was the father. They had given away all but two pups which Frank and Allan had kept for themselves.

"You told me yesterday that you wanted a scout knife more than anything else," I said to Frank. "I'll trade you a scout knife for a pup." I showed him the knife.

He opened all the blades to make sure none were broken. Then he looked at the handle.

"There is a piece of bone missing on the handle," he said.

"What did you expect for a mongrel pup?" I demanded. "A brand new knife? If you don't want to trade, just say so." But I knew from the way he was admiring the knife that I had him.

"I'll trade," he said.

I walked home with him and got the pup. My next stop was Andy Anderson's house. Andy was a boy who had lost his left leg just below the knee. He had a peg leg. He was in their woodshed chopping kindling wood on a chopping block made from the trunk of a tree. He stared at the puppy in my arms.

"Where did you get the pup?" he asked.

"From Frank Jensen," I answered.

He slammed the hatchet into the chopping block. "That ain't fair," he said. "You already got two dogs. I asked Frank and Allan for a pup after my dog died. But they said all the pups were spoken for."

"They were," I said. "This was Frank's own pup. I traded him a scout knife for it. And I'm here to do more trading if you want the pup."

Andy patted the pup on the head. "What do you want for him?" he asked.

"You are getting too big for that wagon of yours," I said. "I'll trade you the pup for the wagon. Then I'm going to trade the wagon to Roger Gillis."

"Boy, you are sure doing a lot of trading," Andy said. "But you are right. I was going to ask for a new wagon for Christmas. Give me the pup and take the wagon."

The next day after school I asked Roger Gillis, who was only seven years old, to come to our barn with me. I showed him the wagon.

"It looks like the one Andy Anderson had," Roger said.

"It is," I said. "I traded him for it."

"What are you going to do with it?" he asked. "You got a wagon and this one is too little for you anyway.

"Remember the air rifle your uncle gave you for your birthday," I said. "You told me your mother put it away and won't let you use it."

"She says I'm too little to have an air rifle," Roger said. "Said I couldn't have it until I was nine or ten years old."

"Then what good is it to you?" I asked. Boy, oh, boy, was I getting to be a sharpie at this trading business. "I'll trade you the wagon for the air rifle. Your mother will probably be glad to get rid of the air rifle if she is so afraid of you using it."

"Let's go ask her," Roger said. And when he picked up the handle of the wagon and began pulling it, I knew I had him.

Mrs. Gillis acted as if I was doing her a big favor trading the wagon for the air rifle. My next stop was in the alley behind the Palace Cafe on the east side of town. Basil Kokovinis lived in an apartment above the cafe with his mother and father. He was helping out in the kitchen when I called to him through the screen door. I remembered Basil telling me that some cowboy had given his father a riding quirt with a short handle and lash of braided rawhide as security for a meal ticket. The cowboy never came back to redeem the riding quirt. It was useless to Basil or his father because they didn't own a horse.

I handed Basil the air rifle when he came to the screen door. "I'll trade you for the riding quirt you told me about," I said.

Basil ran back into the kitchen with the air rifle. I heard him talking half in Greek and half in English with his father. In a few minutes he came out and handed me the riding quirt.

That finished my trading for that day. And I couldn't help thinking that I just might end up becoming the greatest sharpie in Utah someday.

The next morning I talked to Danny Forester, who raised Belgian hare rabbits. When school let out, I traded Danny the riding quirt for a doe rabbit. A short time later I arrived at the home of Parley Benson with the doe in my arms. Parley was in their barn filling the manger with hay for their livestock. He jabbed the pitchfork into a pile of hay when he saw the rabbit in my arms.

"That is a Belgian hare rabbit," he said. "Is it a doe?"

"It's a female," I said. "Just what you said you wanted. I'm here to make a trade."

Parley pushed his coonskin cap to the back of his head. "Just name it," he said. "My doe died, and what good is a buck rabbit without a doe? I tried to get a doe from Danny but he wanted cash and I didn't have enough." He paused, looking puzzled. "Where did you get it?" he asked.

"From Danny," I answered. "I traded him a riding quirt for it. Now I'll trade you the doe for that genuine Indian bow and arrow you own."

"It's a deal," Parley said. "I need the doe more than I do the bow and arrow."

My next stop was the home of Seth Smith. He had just finished dumping a bucketful of slops into the trough in their pigpen. He put the bucket down and stared at the bow and arrow.

"Where did you get the bow and arrow?" he asked. "It's a beauty."

I handed the bow and arrow to him. "You can see for yourself it is a genuine Indian bow and arrow," I said. "I got it from Parley Benson."

Seth admired the bow and tested it. "Boy, I wish it was mine," he said. "What do you want for it, John?"

It never occurred to me until that moment that I didn't know what I wanted for the bow and arrow. Mr. Kramer knew when he started out with his saddle horse that he wanted to end up with a team of mules. I'd known what every kid wanted, and got it for them with my sharp trading. But I didn't know what I wanted. I had just about everything a kid could want.

"What have you got that you'll trade me for it?" I asked Seth.

"How about a knife?" he asked.

"I've got a scout knife," I answered.

"How about some marbles, including my genuine flint taw?" Seth asked.

"I've got all the marbles I need," I said.

One by one Seth named all his worldly possessions. But there wasn't a thing he had that I wanted or needed.

"How about a cash deal?" I asked.

"All I've got is about twelve cents," he said. "I used the rest of the money I had saved up to buy Ma a birthday present."

"Then I guess I'll just have to keep the bow and arrow," I said. "But I don't want it. I've already got one."

Seth looked around desperately until his eye fell on the pigpen. "You ain't got a pig," he said.

"That's right," I said. "I don't own a pig."

Seth motioned for me to follow him and look into the pigpen. "Our sow just finished weaning a litter of piglets," he said. "Pa said I could have one for feeding the pigs. I was going to raise it until it got big enough to sell. I'll trade you a piglet for the bow and arrow. Take your pick of the litter."

I had never fully realized how cute baby pigs were. I leaned over and picked up a little black and white sow.

"You've got yourself a deal," I said.

I couldn't help feeling very proud of myself as a trader as I walked home with the little sow in my arms. I'd started out with just an old Indian suit and war bonnet and now I owned a pig. Then a brilliant idea hit me. Why didn't I go into the pig-raising business? I could raise the little sow until she was old enough to sell for butchering. I'd get enough money to buy about three weanling pigs. And I'd raise them until they were old enough to sell. But I'd only sell two of them and buy a boar. Then I'd breed my sow to the boar. And that would give me a litter of pigs. In no time at all I'd own a lot of pigs. I would keep breeding them and selling them and make a fortune. Even Tom with his great brain never came up with a brilliant idea for making money like this. I'd put the little sow in the barn for tonight. Tomorrow after school I'd get some wooden crates from Mr. Harmon at the Z.C.M.I. store and build a pigpen. I was so proud of myself, I just had to show Mamma the little sow before I put her in the barn.

Mamma and Aunt Bertha were starting to prepare supper in the kitchen. Mamma put her hands on her hips as she always did when angry.

"John Dennis, just what do you think you are doing with that pig?" she demanded.

I couldn't understand why she was angry. I knew as soon as I told her about all the sharp trading I had done that she would be proud of me. And I knew she'd be even prouder when I told her about my plans to go into the pig-raising business. So I told her and Aunt Bertha all about it, right from the beginning. It was strange but the more they listened, the angrier Mamma looked.

"What is the matter with you, Mamma?" I asked as I finished. "You look angry when you should look proud for having such a shrewd and clever son. I'm going to raise pigs and make a lot of money."

"Well, you certainly aren't going to raise them around here," Mamma said sharply. "I do not mind horses. I do not mind a milk cow. I do not mind chickens. But there is one thing I will never permit and that is a pigpen in our backyard. Now just march yourself back to Seth Smith and give him back his pig."

"But Mamma . . ." I started to protest.

"There are no buts, and there will be no pigs," Mamma said firmly. "You get rid of that pig and do it right now."

Boy, oh, boy, what a disaster this was after all my sharp trading. I knew there was never any appealing one of Mamma's decisions. I went back to Seth's house, and found him practicing with the bow and arrow in his backyard.

"Trade me back," I said. "My mother won't let me keep the sow."

"A trade is a trade," Seth said.

"But my mother says I can't keep the pig," I protested. "What can I do with it?"

Seth thought for a moment. "Maybe I could board the sow for you until it got big enough to sell," he said.

"That is a peach of an idea," I said, feeling mighty relieved. "How much will it cost?"

"Growing pigs eat a lot," he said. "I figure it will cost you about ten cents a week."

He had me over a barrel and knew it. "All right," I said. "I'll pay you when I sell it."

Seth shook his head. "Nope," he said. "What if she gets sick and dies? You will have to pay in advance every week."

I sure as heck wasn't going to be paying ten cents a week to Seth and then have the pig die on me before she was old enough to sell.

"I won't pay in advance," I said.

"It is your sow," he said. "I don't care what you do with it. But I might do you a favor and take it off your hands, seeing as how your Ma won't let you keep it."

"And I won't have to pay ten cents a week?" I asked.

"Nope," Seth said, "providing you give me back the pig and I get to keep the bow and arrow."

"It's a deal," I said. I handed the little sow to Seth and watched him put it back in the pigpen.

As I walked home I wondered if Mr. Kramer had ever ended up on the short end of a trade the way I had. I didn't think so. There was more to this trading business than I had thought. One thing I knew for sure. This was going to be the end of my trading days.

Mamma, of course, had to tell Papa all about it during supper. I sure didn't think it was funny, but it made Papa laugh.

"I guess, J.D.," he said, "that you got the idea from Alex Kramer."

"And I guess, Papa," I said, "that I'm just a born loser."

Papa stopped laughing. His face became serious and so did his voice. "There is no such a thing as a born loser," he said. "But there are people who continually overreach themselves. And when they fail to achieve their objective, they call themselves born losers and wallow in self-pity."

"I don't quite understand," I said.

"Every person on this earth is limited to what they can do in life by what is called inherent talent and native ability," Papa said. "This determines what each person can do best. One man might have the inherent ability to become a great musician while another couldn't become a great musician if he practiced all his life."

"How do you know what you can do best?" I asked.

"A great burning desire to become something is a good indication a person has the ability for it," Papa said. "A man who has this desire to become a doctor or lawyer or journalist or merchant or teacher or farmer and so on almost always achieves his goal. And it is this gift of birth that divides people into all the vocations that are needed for mankind to survive. But there are some people who stifle this desire to be something they can be. They are motivated by admiration or envy to try to be something else. For example, J.D., you were motivated by admiration for Alex Kramer to become a trader, although you lacked the ability to be a successful trader. As a result you failed."

Papa leaned back in his chair. "And while we are on the subject," he said, "I think it is high time you stopped trying to imitate your brother Tom. I know your admiration for him has made you try to take his place. But you lack the

36

shrewdness of your brother, so you can never even come close to taking his place. Find your own identity and say to yourself, this is me, and I can't be anybody but me. Know thyself and be thyself. That is the key to a happy and well-adjusted life."

At first I thought that Papa was telling me in a polite way that I was pretty darn dumb. I'd got nine kids things they wanted and what did I get out of it? Absolutely nothing. And when Tom found out I'd traded away his old Indian suit and war bonnet, he would probably claim they were priceless heirlooms or something and charge me plenty.

But the more I thought about what Papa had told me, the more convinced I became that he wasn't just telling me I was dumb. What he said about being yourself made sense. And I figured the best way to begin to know myself was by admitting that I only had a little brain, and the best way to start being myself was to stop trying to imitate my brother Tom.

CHAPTER THREE

Frankie Pennyworth

I FIGURED NOW THAT I'd learned to know myself and just be myself that all my troubles were over. I was looking forward to the "happy and well-adjusted life" Papa had promised me. I began by telling Frank and Allan Jensen that I'd do my own chores from now on. I talked this over with Papa first. He was pleased I'd given up trying to imitate Tom but worried about Frank and Allan not having any spending money. He solved the problem by hiring them for ten cents a week to deliver the *Advocate* every Tuesday after school.

Everything went along just dandy for a couple of weeks. I was enjoying just being me and Papa said I was on the right road. Then I discovered that a fellow could be on the right road himself but somebody else on another road could change his whole life for him.

The road that ruined my happy and well-adjusted life was the old road up Red Rock Canyon to the plateau and over the mountain. This had been the main road to Silverlode when it was a booming mining town, and to Adenville from Cedar City. After Silverlode became a ghost town, a railroad was built from Cedar City to Adenville and the towns south. Then a new road for wagons was built alongside the railroad tracks. It was a longer route, but a much better and safer one to travel. The old road up Red Rock Canyon had always been dangerous due to rock and land slides, especially after a heavy rain. Papa told me one time that when it was the main road people were killed in Red Rock Canyon almost every week.

The only people who used the road now were a few homesteaders who lived on the plateau, and trappers and hunters. It was this road that brought Frankie Pennyworth into my life. His name should have been Frankenstein Dollarworth because he was a monster and a dollar's worth of trouble. I know that sounds impossible when I tell you that Frankie was only four years old. But I'd better start at the beginning.

Mr. Pennyworth, his wife, and two sons named William and Frank lived on the plateau, where they had a homestead of one hundred and sixty acres. They grew mostly wheat, which Mr. Pennyworth sold to the flour mill in Adenville. During the winter months Mr. Pennyworth worked as a trapper and brought his cache of furs into Adenville to sell. His son William was ten years old but never attended school in Adenville because it was too far to travel.

Uncle Mark came to our house about seven o'clock on a Friday evening carrying Frankie Pennyworth in his arms. The boy was asleep. There was mud on Frankie's clothing and all over Uncle Mark. This surprised me because it hadn't rained a drop in town all day. But I did notice it was raining on the plateau and in the mountains.

"Good Lord, Mark!" Mamma exclaimed when she opened the front door. "What happened to you and who is that boy?"

"His name is Frankie Pennyworth," Uncle Mark said, after wiping his feet on the doormat and coming into the parlor. "His parents and brother were killed by a rock and land slide in Red Rock Canyon. I would have taken him home with me, but as you know Cathie is back east visiting relatives. I didn't know what else to do so I brought him here."

"Explanations can wait," Mamma said. She took the boy in her arms, unmindful of the mud on his clothes. "Bertha, go up to the attic and get one of John D.'s old nightgowns and a robe. I'll give the little fellow a sponge bath and put him to bed. I'll let him sleep with me tonight because he'll be frightened when he wakes up."

"Try not to wake him while you are putting him to bed," Uncle Mark said. "Doctor LeRoy said the longer he sleeps the better."

Mamma left the parlor with Frankie and Aunt Bertha.

"What happened?" Papa asked.

Uncle Mark removed his Stetson hat, but remained standing because his clothes were so muddy. His face was very grim. He told us that the Pennyworths had left their farm early that morning to drive into Adenville for supplies.

They had stopped at the farmhouse of another homesteader named Parker to get a list of supplies the Parker family needed. It was about a two-hour trip from the plateau to Adenville. When six hours passed without the Pennyworths returning, Mr. Parker saddled a horse and started down the canyon. About two-thirds of the way down he came upon a gigantic rock and land slide that covered the road to a depth of almost a hundred feet and for a distance of about a quarter of a mile. He saw no sign of life and thought the Pennyworths might have passed before the slide and when they tried to come back had to return to Adenville. He rode his horse up the side of the mountain around the slide and came into town. Upon discovering the Pennyworths had never arrived in Adenville, he went to the Marshal's office to tell Uncle Mark.

"I arranged for some men with wagons and shovels to follow us," Uncle Mark said, "and then rode to the scene of the slide with Mr. Parker. I knew it was hopeless the minute I saw the slide. It looked as if half the mountain had dropped on the road and bottom of the canyon. It would take an army of men weeks, and maybe even months, to find the bodies under all those tons and tons of rock and dirt. That is the end of Red Rock Canyon road. It will be impossible to build another road over that slide. The people on the plateau will have to go all the way down the other side of the mountain for supplies from now on."

"But the boy is alive," Papa said.

"We thought for sure the entire family were buried under the slide," Uncle Mark said. "I rode to the other side of it with Mr. Parker. We found no signs of life. Then Mr. Parker said he had to be getting on home. And he promised to look out for the milk cow and chickens on the Pennyworth farm. He started up the road. I was getting ready to ride back to the other side of the slide to meet the men coming with wagons. I heard Parker shout at me. I turned and saw him riding toward me holding Frankie on his saddle. He said he'd missed seeing Frankie earlier because the boy was under a ledge by the side of the road."

"Didn't the boy tell you what had happened?" Papa asked.

"He couldn't," Uncle Mark said. "He is in a state of shock. He hasn't cried one tear or said one word since we found him. I brought him back on my horse with me and tried to get him to talk but he wouldn't. He went to sleep just before we got to town. I took him to Doctor LeRoy. The doctor examined him and said there was no concussion or bruises. He said the boy was in a deep sleep from shock exhaustion. How the boy escaped and the others didn't we won't know until Frankie comes out of his shock and can tell us."

"I know you must be tired, Mark," Papa said. "You go on home. I'll tell Tena and Bertha all about it."

"Parker is going to notify friends of the Pennyworths on the plateau," Uncle Mark said. "I will meet them at the upper side of the slide tomorrow morning with Reverend Holcomb, who will hold a funeral service there. Good night."

"Good night," Papa and I both said.

Uncle Mark had just left when Mamma and Aunt Bertha came back into the parlor. Papa told them what we had learned from Uncle Mark about the accident. Mamma didn't even know the Pennyworths and neither did Aunt Bertha, but they both began to cry.

It was past my bedtime so I went up to my room. I fell asleep feeling very sorry for a four-year-old boy who had lost his parents and brother. The next thing I knew I was having a nightmare. I dreamt an Indian had sneaked into my room and was beating me on the head with a tomahawk. I woke up. It was daylight. But I was still being hit on the head. I was so stunned that I just lay there as a very hard wallop landed on my left ear. I turned over on my back. I could see a hand with my shoe in it. The shoe came down and hit me so hard on the nose that it started to bleed. I grabbed the shoe and sat up in bed. And who do you think was standing beside my bed in my old nightgown waking me up by pounding on my head with a shoe? Nobody else but Frankie Pennyworth. I took the shoe away from him and jumped out of bed.

"Why did you do that?" I demanded. "And how come you are upstairs instead of in Mamma's bedroom?"

He folded his arms on his chest. His big dark eyes beneath his black head of hair just glared at me as if he hated the sight of me.

"Answer me!" I shouted, feeling blood from my nose running over my lips.

He answered me all right. He bent over and picked up my other shoe and banged me on my bare toes so hard it made me cry out with pain. I grabbed that shoe and took it away from him.

"What kind of a loco kid are you?" I cried. I was so angry I was about to box his ears when Mamma called up the stairway.

"Is Frankie up there, John D.?"

"He is up here and tried to murder me in my sleep!" I answered.

43

Mamma came rushing upstairs and picked Frankie up in her arms. She got punched right on the nose for it. She stared at him with astonishment.

"Don't let a little thing like that bother you," I said. "He was pounding me on the head with my shoe when I woke up."

"Your nose is bleeding and so is your ear," Mamma said.

"He is crazy, Mamma," I said. "What happened to him must have driven him plumb loco."

Frankie proved I was right by trying to gouge Mamma's eyes with his fingers. She then held him so he couldn't move his arms.

"Don't be a naughty boy, Frankie," she said. "We are your friends and love you. And to prove it you can have anything you want for breakfast."

This kid was unbelievable. Instead of thanking Mamma, he began kicking her. He didn't say one word or let out one peep as she held him tight and carried him downstairs.

I went down to the bathroom, where I put cold towels on the back of my neck until my nose stopped bleeding. Then I put some peroxide and a bandage on my ear. I could hear Mamma pleading with Frankie in her bedroom as she tried to get him dressed in some of my old clothes. I went back upstairs and got dressed. Breakfast wasn't ready when I came down so I went into the parlor. Papa was there.

"What happened to your ear?" he asked.

I told him about Frankie trying to beat me to death. But did I get any sympathy? Heck, no.

"How unusual," was all Papa said.

Then Mamma brought Frankie into the parlor dressed in one of my old Buster Brown suits. "I'll leave Frankie with you while I help Bertha with breakfast," she said.

Frankie stood with his arms folded on his chest looking

at Papa as if he would enjoy seeing him boiled in oil. Then he walked over and kicked Papa on the shin. Papa lifted up his leg and grabbed his shin.

"Now you stop that, Frankie," he said.

It was a stupid thing to tell a kid who was plumb loco. Frankie kicked Papa on the other shin. Papa hadn't given me any sympathy and I wasn't about to give him any.

"How unusual," I said.

I was so intent on watching Papa rub both his shins that I wasn't paying any attention to Frankie. The little monster walked over and kicked me on the shin so hard it really hurt. Then he sat down on the floor with his arms on his chest and glared at us as if we were his worst enemies.

"This kid belongs in a cell down at the jail," I said.

Did Papa telephone Uncle Mark to come get the little monster and lock him up in jail? Heck, no.

"This is very interesting," Papa said.

Boy, oh, boy, I never knew being beaten on the head and toes with a shoe and being kicked on the shins was interesting.

In a few minutes Mamma came into the parlor and told us breakfast was ready. She tried to pick Frankie up in her arms. He punched and kicked her so hard she had to put him down.

"Now be a good boy, Frankie," she pleaded. "I know you must be hungry. You can have a nice bowl of oatmeal. And you can have some nice hot cakes with maple syrup or sugar on them."

Again she tried to pick him up. This time he not only punched and kicked her but tried to scratch her eyes out. She had to let go of him.

46

Aunt Bertha came into the parlor. "Things are getting cold," she said.

"Frankie won't let me touch him," Mamma said, looking completely bewildered.

Aunt Bertha looked at Frankie. "Now let's not have any more nonsense," she said. "Breakfast is ready, Frankie, and you are going to eat."

I'll be a four-eyed frog if Frankie didn't hold out his arms toward Aunt Bertha. He didn't kick or punch as she picked him up. She carried him to the kitchen and put him in a chair.

"Very interesting," Papa said as he sat down at the table.

It got even more interesting when Mamma put a bowl of oatmeal in front of him. Frankie picked it up and threw it on the floor.

"Clean it up later," Papa said. "Now let Bertha give him a bowl."

Aunt Bertha fixed a bowl of oatmeal and put sugar and cream on it. She put it in front of him and handed Frankie a spoon. I watched, bug-eyed, as Frankie started eating the oatmeal as if he were starved.

Papa waited until we had all eaten our cereal. "Now, Tena," he said, "you give Frankie a glass of milk."

Mamma poured a glass of milk from the pitcher and gave it to Frankie. I'll bet she wished she hadn't when Frankie threw the glass of milk on the floor.

"Let the mess go," Papa said. "My theory is proving itself. Now, Bertha, you give him a glass of milk."

Aunt Bertha poured a glass of milk and put it in front of him. Frankie picked up the glass and drank all the milk in it.

"I think, Bertha," Papa said, "that you had better serve Frankie his hot cakes."

Mamma appeared to be completely bewildered. "I don't understand," she said. "I've never known a child who didn't like me."

"I'll explain later," Papa said.

We finished eating our breakfast, with Frankie eating three hot cakes and drinking another glass of milk served to him by Aunt Bertha. Papa then asked her to take Frankie into the parlor for a few minutes. Frankie put his arms around her neck and held her tight when she picked him up. He gave the rest of us a real nasty look as if he despised us.

"You said you had a theory," Mamma said after Aunt Bertha and Frankie had left the kitchen.

"The boy recognizes that you are the mother and I am the father and J.D. is the son in this house," Papa said. "When he woke up this morning he went looking for his own parents and brother. Instead he found us. He also found himself in a strange house. He is still in a state of shock. And I think he believes that we did away with his own parents and brother so we could take their places. That is why he hates us three. He has no such association with Bertha because he evidently didn't have an aunt."

"Poor little fellow," Mamma cried. "How long do you think it will be until he gets over it?"

"I have no idea," Papa said. "But I do know I've read of people who have undergone such a horrible experience that they get a mental block. In other words the shock is so great that their minds refuse to remember the experience. I'll talk to Dr. LeRoy about it today. Meanwhile, all we can do is to give Frankie all the love and understanding possible."

48

"You mean we just let him go on hitting us and kicking us whenever he wants?" I asked.

"The boy is temporarily mentally disturbed," Papa said. "He is not responsible for his actions."

"Boy, oh, boy, he'll get by with murder," I protested, "Aren't you even going to give him the silent treatment?"

Papa and Mamma never whipped my brothers or me when we did something wrong. Instead they gave us the silent treatment, which was worse than a whipping. For a period of a day or a week or even longer neither one of them would speak to us. And they would pretend they didn't hear if we spoke to them.

Papa thumped his finger on the table to emphasize each word as he spoke. "I told you the boy is not responsible for anything he does," he said firmly. "And don't you forget that, J.D., or you will be the one getting the silent treatment."

I excused myself and got up from the table. "I am going to do my morning chores and then go play with the kids," I said.

"You will do your chores," Mamma said. "And then you will spend the rest of the day trying to make friends with Frankie. Get some of the games you used to like to play when his age out of the attic and play with him."

"The only game that kid would like to play with me is to beat me black and blue," I protested.

"You will do as you are told," Mamma said, "and not another word out of you. And he isn't 'that kid' but Frankie."

I did as I had been told. I finished my chores and went up to the attic. I looked in a box where Mamma had stored all the games my brothers and I used to play. I finally decided on a set of logs and blocks that could be made into a log cabin. I remembered how I used to like to build the log cabin when I was about Frankie's age. Then I went to my room and got my catcher's mask and put it on. I was no dummy.

I went down to the kitchen, where Frankie was watching Mamma and Aunt Bertha preparing to bake some cookies.

"There will be no ball-playing for you today," Mamma said sternly. "Take off that catcher's mask right now. I told you to play with Frankie."

"I didn't put it on to play ball," I said. "I put it on to play with Frankie. You can give me the silent treatment for a year but I'm not going to play with him without some protection."

"All right," Mamma said. "Take him into the parlor."

Frankie ran over and grabbed hold of Aunt Bertha's skirt. He wouldn't budge until she took him by the hand and led him into the parlor.

"Your Aunt Bertha wants you to sit on the floor and play with John," she said.

Frankie nodded his head. He obeyed her and sat down. But he stared at me as if he'd like to cut my throat.

"I'll show you how to build a log cabin," I said as I dumped the blocks and logs from the box.

He watched me build the log cabin. I let him look at it for a moment and then knocked it down.

"Now see if you can build a log cabin," I said.

He picked up one of the blocks and threw it straight at my face. It hit my catcher's mask and fell to the floor.

"Ha, ha," I said. I wanted this little monster to know I was too smart for him.

That really made him angry. He began throwing blocks and logs at me. They bounced harmlessly off my catcher's

50

mask because they were all too big to go through the holes in the mask. Then one of the blocks went sailing over my head. It hit one of the glass doors on the bookcase and cracked the glass.

"Mamma!" I shouted. "You had better come in here if you don't want the furniture wrecked."

Mamma and Aunt Bertha arrived in the parlor just as the last piece of the log cabin bounced off my catcher's mask. Frankie folded his arms on his chest and stuck out his lower lip as if he'd like to take a bite out of me.

I stood up. "You see, Mamma," I said, "if I hadn't been wearing my catcher's mask I'd be blind in both eyes now and my face would be cut to ribbons. A fellow could get killed playing with this kid."

"Stop exaggerating," Mamma said. "And I'm not going to tell you again to stop calling Frankie 'this kid.' The next time it will cost you one week's allowance."

"In other words," I protested, "I'm just to let him murder me. And when you see your youngest son lying dead in a coffin then maybe you'll be sorry."

"Stop being melodramatic," Mamma said. "Play some other game with him, like checkers."

"Not me," I said. "Checkers are small enough to go through the holes in my catcher's mask."

"Then play tiddlywinks with him," Mamma said. "I'm sure those little chips can't hurt you. And I don't want one more word out of you about it."

I knew if I opened my mouth I'd lose a week's allowance. I did get some satisfaction when Mamma tried to pat Frankie on the head. He grabbed her hand and bit it. Then just to show he didn't hate Aunt Bertha, he walked over and took her hand and kissed it.

Frankie must have learned how to play tiddlywinks with his brother because he knew how to play. He did throw the leather cup at me a couple of times. He gave up when he saw it bounce harmlessly off my catcher's mask. Then he stopped playing the game. He reached over and pinched me on the leg. He sure had a lot of strength for a four year old. He pinched me hard enough to make my leg turn black and blue. I decided I needed more protection. I went up to my room and put on my football suit. It had padded pants and padded shoulders. I really needed a suit of armor but the football suit would have to do.

I don't believe Frankie had ever seen a football suit. When I came back into the parlor he was standing in the middle of the room. I walked over beside him and turned my head away. He grabbed my leg and pinched it but the padding protected me. I laughed at him. This made him try to bite me on the leg, but again the padding protected me. I figured I had him completely buffaloed when he walked over by the fireplace and stood there glaring at me, his fists clenched by his sides.

I sat down with my back toward him and began putting the tiddlywinks into the leather cup. Suddenly I saw stars. I got to my feet. Frankie had taken a big stick of wood from the fireplace woodbox and belted me on the head with it. I let out a yell that brought Mamma and Aunt Bertha into the parlor.

"He tried to kill me!" I shouted. I pointed at Frankie, who still held the stick of wood in his hand.

Aunt Bertha held out her hand. Frankie gave her the stick of wood without any protest.

Mamma shook her head sadly. "So much hatred and all

misdirected," she said. "You will just have to watch him the best you can, John D. Bertha and I have baking to do."

"Not until I get my football helmet," I said.

When I returned wearing my football helmet, Mamma and Aunt Bertha left me alone with Frankie. I figured if he'd never seen a football suit that he had never seen a football helmet. I picked up a stick of wood from the woodbox and handed it to him. Then I got down on my knees and bent my head over.

"Go ahead and sock me, you little monster," I challenged him.

He belted me a couple of times on the football helmet. I laughed at him to let him know he wasn't hurting me a bit. This made him so angry that he threw down the stick and walked over and climbed up on the couch. He folded his arms on his chest and stared at me as if wishing he had a cage of hungry lions to throw me into.

This suited me fine. I sat down in Papa's rocking chair and stared right back at him. We were sitting like that when Papa came home early for lunch. Frankie greeted Papa by running over and kicking him on the shins. Papa just shook his head sadly and moved far enough away so Frankie couldn't kick him again.

"What are you all dressed up for?" he asked.

"This is the only way I can protect myself from Frankie," I answered.

"I am beginning to see what you mean, J.D.," Papa said. "I came home early for lunch because I want to talk to your mother. Ask Bertha to take Frankie into the kitchen."

CHAPTER FOUR

Curing Frankie's Mental Block

PAPA SAT DOWN IN HIS rocking chair after Aunt Bertha had taken Frankie into the kitchen. Mamma and I remained standing.

"Mark left this morning with Reverend Holcomb to hold a funeral service at the slide," Papa said. "Mr. Harmon and some other people in town who did business with Mr. Pennyworth went along. The Parker family and other friends of the Pennyworths living on the plateau will meet them at the slide. After the service Mark will go to the Pennyworth farm and see if he can find any letters or anything that will help him locate relatives who would take Frankie. However, Mr. Parker told Mark he had never heard the Pennyworths mention having any close living relatives."

"I am more interested in what Dr. LeRoy had to say," Mamma said. "The hatred in that little boy for the three of us is unbelievable."

"He agrees with my theory," Papa said.

"Then we must place the boy in another home until Mark locates some relatives," Mamma said.

"I suggested that to Dr. LeRoy," Papa said. "He doesn't think it would make any difference. The boy would just transfer his hatred to the new family. Dr. LeRoy also believes that the boy will not recover until he lets all that grief and terror bottled up inside him come out. Frankie can't do that until he can cry and talk. And he can't cry and talk until he remembers the accident and what really happened to his parents and brother."

"Did the doctor give you any indication of just how long that might be?" Mamma asked.

"No," Papa answered. "He said it could happen in a day or a week, or Frankie might not get over it for a long time, unless he had expert medical help."

I sure didn't want to live in the same house with the little monster for months. "Boy, oh, boy," I said, "I sure hope Uncle Mark finds some relatives quick before Frankie drives us all crazy or murders us in our sleep."

"Stop talking nonsense," Papa reprimanded me.

Mamma apparently didn't think it was nonsense. "Let us assume that Mark is unable to locate any relatives," she said.

Papa looked at her for a moment before answering. "You mean, what will we do if no relatives are located who will take the boy and if he doesn't recover his memory in a week or so?"

"Yes," Mamma answered.

"I asked myself and the doctor that very same question," Papa said. "Dr. LeRoy hasn't the medical education to treat a mental patient. However, he knows of a doctor in Salt Lake City named Lieberman who has a private sanitarium and specializes in treating mental patients. I will take Frankie there." Papa inhaled and exhaled deeply as he shook his head. "If the boy would only cry and let out what is bottled up inside him, it would solve everything."

I took off my football helmet and rubbed the bump on my head. "I'll gladly take on the job of making him cry," I said.

That sure made Papa angry. "I'm giving you an order right now, J.D. Don't you dare lay a hand on that boy no matter what he does to you. And you'd better start right this minute thinking of him as a helpless little boy who needs all the love and understanding you can give him."

I knew Papa and Mamma were determined to think of Frankie as a helpless little boy until he cut all our throats. If they had taken the abuse I'd taken, they would know the accident had turned him into a homicidal maniac. They could think what they wanted, but I was going to be on my guard day and night. I'd not only lock my bedroom door at night but also push the dresser up against it.

I had to take off my catcher's mask to eat lunch but I made sure I sat far enough away from Frankie that he couldn't stab me with a knife or fork. The meal was peaceful enough, with Aunt Bertha serving Frankie all of his food, until Mamma forgot and tried to give the boy a second piece of cake. He rapped her across the knuckles so hard with his fork it made her drop the cake. He ate a second piece that Aunt Bertha served him.

I'd been doing some thinking during lunch. If I was going to take a chance of being crippled or killed, I figured I should be paid for it. I wasn't trying to imitate Tom. I was just being me and using my common sense. I walked to the front porch with Papa after lunch.

"Mamma has given me orders to play with Frankie," I said. "I'm taking my life in my hands but I'll do it. And it means I won't get to play with the other kids and have any fun at all."

"I think I know what you are leading up to," Papa said. "If your Uncle Mark doesn't locate any relatives, we will keep Frankie with us for one week. As a boy maybe you can get closer to Frankie than the rest of us. You do everything you can to make him well during that week and if you succeed I'll give you a dollar. The rest of us will give you all the help we possibly can."

"Boy, oh, boy!" I shouted joyfully.

"Not so fast," Papa said. "If I have to take Frankie to Dr. Lieberman in Salt Lake City at the end of that week, you get nothing."

"But that isn't fair," I protested.

"I think it is, for the following reason," Papa said. "It will make you try twice as hard to win Frankie's confidence and friendship and help him get well."

I started earning that dollar right away. Mamma told me that I'd have to mind Frankie because she and Aunt Bertha had work to do. I thought if I took Frankie outside it would make it easier. I had on my football suit and my catcher's mask and football helmet just in case. I figured even a kid with a mental block must like dogs.

I whistled for my dogs as Frankie and I came down the

steps of our back porch. Both of them came running from the rear of the yard. Then a horrible thought hit me. I wasn't afraid of my dogs biting Frankie, but what if the little monster tried to bite them? I patted Brownie and Prince on their heads. Then the pup ran over to Frankie, wagging his tail and barking.

Frankie looked down at Prince for a moment. Then he dropped to his knees and began petting and hugging him. I wasn't taking any chances. I watched closely to make sure Frankie didn't try to strangle the pup. But he played with Prince just like a normal kid.

I had taught both my dogs to fetch a stick or a ball. I picked up a stick and threw it. Brownie ran and got it and brought it back to me. Frankie watched me do this a couple of times. Then he picked up a stick and threw it. Prince ran and got it and brought it back to Frankie. I figured Frankie would go on playing with Prince, and got careless. I sat down with my back toward Frankie and began scratching Brownie behind the ears. I could hear Prince barking and assumed he was still fetching sticks for Frankie. A few minutes later there was a thumping sound on my football helmet. I turned around.

Frankie had gathered up a pile of rocks and was throwing them at me. I guess I felt safe with my catcher's mask on because I just sat there. It was a stupid thing to do. Frankie threw a sharp pointed rock that was small enough to go through the holes in my catcher's mask. I could feel blood running down my cheek as I got up and went into the kitchen.

Mamma was greasing a bread pan with a piece of bacon rind. "Your cheek!" she cried.

"Frankie hit me with a rock that went through my

mask," I said. I sure didn't want to tell her I'd been dumb enough to just sit there and let him do it.

"Come into the bathroom and let me fix it," Mamma said, wiping her hands on her apron.

I took off my football helmet and catcher's mask and followed her into the bathroom. She bathed the cut on my cheek with peroxide and then put a bandage on it. I was surprised to see tears come into her eyes. It really didn't hurt me enough to make her cry over it.

"I love you very much, John D.," Mamma said. "I would never forgive myself if anything happened to you because of Frankie. I didn't tell you but he tried to steal a paring knife after lunch while you were talking to your father on the front porch. And although you exaggerated about how dangerous he was, there is a great deal of truth in what you said. I am going to insist that your father take him to Doctor Lieberman in Salt Lake City."

I thought about the dollar Papa had promised me. I could kiss it good-bye unless I thought fast.

"Please don't, Mamma," I pleaded. "Please wait at least for a week."

She looked surprised. "There is something going on I don't know about," she said. "Fess up, John D. What is it?"

"Papa promised me a dollar if I could help make Frankie well in a week," I said.

Mamma shook her head. "I am sorry, son, but the boy is too dangerous to keep here for a week," she said. "I'm afraid Frankie needs the sort of help only Doctor Lieberman can give him. I'll have your father take him to Salt Lake City on the Monday morning train. Until then I will have Bertha take care of him during the day. And your father, Bertha, and I will take turns watching him during the night."

"But Papa has to get out his newspaper," I protested. "And why not wait until we find out if Frankie has some relatives?"

"My mind is made up," Mamma said with determination. "Meanwhile, you are not to play with Frankie. I'll have Bertha take care of him. And you are to stay far enough away from him so he cannot harm you. Is that understood, John D.?"

In every court in the country anybody can appeal a decision right up to the Supreme Court of the United States. But no kid in the whole United States can appeal any decision his mother makes.

I followed Mamma into the kitchen. Aunt Bertha wasn't there. We found her sitting on the back porch holding Frankie in her lap.

"Bertha," Mamma said. "Tell Frankie he must remain on the porch. Come into the kitchen. There is something I want to discuss with you."

Aunt Bertha put Frankie down. "You stay right on this porch," she said to him.

I could tell by the look on his face that he didn't like it. But he folded his arms on his chest and sat in the old chair on our back porch.

I went to the barn and climbed up the rope ladder to Tom's loft. Mamma had ordered me not to play with Frankie or get near enough to him to get hurt in any way. This was one place I felt perfectly safe. I sure hated to lose that dollar Papa had promised me. I lay down on my stomach to think about it. The more I thought about it the more convinced I became that Mamma was right. When a fellow tries to protect himself with a football suit and helmet and a catcher's mask and still gets hurt, it is time to give up. I was now convinced that the accident had turned Frankie into a maniac who wouldn't rest until he'd killed Papa, Mamma, and me.

I was lying on my stomach facing the top of the rope ladder when I though for sure I was having a daymare, or whatever they call a nightmare that you have in the daytime. I saw the black hair first and then the big dark eyes. And I'll be a four-eyed bullfrog if I wasn't staring right into Frankie's face. I hadn't been able to climb up the rope ladder until I was five years old. I was so sure it was a dream that I reached out and touched him on the head. Then I knew I wasn't dreaming.

I started to tell him to climb back down the ladder but didn't. I was afraid he would fall. It is always harder to go down a ladder than to go up because you have to watch your feet. I reached down and got hold of him under the armpits and lifted him onto the loft. Then I sat down on a box and just stared at him. He walked around the loft looking at things and touching them. He even touched the skull of the Indian. I kept an eye on him so he couldn't pick up something and throw it at me. I knew I had to get him down from the loft. Although Aunt Bertha was supposed to be watching him, if anything happened to him it would be my fault. I waited until he had seen everything in the loft and sat down on a box.

"Frankie," I said, "Aunt Bertha will be worried about you. And it is time for her to give you a glass of milk and some cookies. You climb on my back and put your arms around my neck and hold on tight. I'll carry you down the rope ladder."

He got up and walked to the edge of the loft and looked down. I guess he was wondering if he should try to climb down the ladder by himself. Then he got on my back and put his arms around my neck. I carried him down the rope ladder. He let go and dropped to the ground. He thanked me by kicking me on the shins. I grabbed his hand and pulled him out of the barn.

"Now you beat it back to Aunt Bertha," I ordered him.

He just folded his arms on his chest and glared at me. I ran back into the barn. I climbed up the rope ladder as quickly as I could. Then I pulled the rope ladder up to the loft. I made it just in time. I looked over the edge. Frankie came into the barn and stood staring up at the loft.

"You can't get at me now, you little monster," I shouted at him. "Maybe I'll just live up here until Papa takes you to Salt Lake City."

I lay down on my back and stared up at the roof. It wasn't a bad idea at that. Mamma could give me a couple of blankets and a pillow. She could put my meals in a bucket and I could haul it up with Sweyn's lariat. I heard our milk cow start mooing. I looked over the edge of the loft again.

Frankie had the barn door open. He was leading our milk cow out of the barn. That didn't worry me. I figured he was taking the cow to the water trough in the corral for a drink of water. In a couple of minutes he came back and led Sweyn's mustang, Dusty, out of the barn. Then he came back and led our team of horses out. I knew he'd been raised on a farm and thought he probably helped his brother water their livestock. And I knew our own livestock couldn't get out of the corral. So it didn't bother me.

But I did become worried when I heard Brownie barking. It was an alarm bark. Any boy who owns a dog can tell the difference in the way his dog barks. It might be a happy bark like when you are playing with him. It might be an excited bark like when you are rabbit-hunting and he sees a rabbit. It might be a thank-you bark when you feed him. And there are many other kinds of barks a kid will recognize. I knew Brownie's bark was an alarm bark. He was telling me something was wrong. I climbed down the rope ladder and ran out of the barn. My dog was sure right. The corral gate was open. Our milk cow, the team of horses, and Dusty were all gone. We had a chicken run made from wire fence because Mamma didn't like chickens running all over our yard. The gate was open. Frankie was chasing all the chickens out of the chicken run.

I knew I'd get the blame for all this even though Aunt Bertha was supposed to be watching Frankie. It would take me a long time to round up our livestock and all the chickens. I thought about this and all the things Frankie had done to me. Then I got a mental block of my own. I was so angry I could actually see red, and in the middle of that red was Frankie. I ran over and grabbed him by the wrist as he was coming out of the gate of the chicken run.

"Now you are going to get it!" I said. "Papa and Mamma will give me the silent treatment for a month for letting the livestock and chickens get out. And they will take away my allowance for a year for what I'm going to do for you. But I don't care. It will be worth it to teach you a lesson, you little monster."

He began to kick and fight. I dragged him into our woodshed. I picked up a flat piece of kindling wood to use as a paddle. I sat down on the chopping block and threw him over my knees. I let him have a hard whack on the behind with the paddle. "That was for hitting me on the head with my shoe," I said.

I gave him another hard whack. "That was for kicking me on the shins," I said.

I gave him another good whack. "That was for kicking me on the shins," I said.

I gave him another whack. "That was for belting me on the head with the stick of firewood," I said.

Then I gave him three hard whacks in a row. "That was for throwing rocks at me," I said.

Frankie let out a scream. That made me feel good because I knew I was hurting the little monster.

I gave him three more hard whacks while he screamed bloody murder. "That was for letting the livestock and chickens out," I said.

He was really bawling as I gave him three more whacks just in case I'd forgotten anything. Then I let him go.

He ran crying and yelling out of the woodshed. I walked out after him. Mamma and Aunt Bertha had heard him and were running toward the woodshed, Aunt Bertha in the lead.

"John spanked me!" Frankie screamed.

Aunt Bertha stooped over and held out her arms. Frankie ran right by her and into Mamma's arms, carrying on as if I'd tried to murder him.

It took me more than an hour to round up the livestock and chickens. Then it was time to go inside and discover what my punishment would be for spanking Frankie.

I walked to the back porch and into the kitchen. It was empty. I could hear Papa's voice in the parlor and I thought Mamma must not have been able to wait till suppertime for him to hand down his punishment. She must have telephoned him and told him I'd spanked Frankie. I squared my shoulders. I felt like a man going to face a firing squad as I walked into the parlor.

64

Mamma was sitting in her maple rocker holding Frankie on her lap. Papa was sitting in his rocking chair. Aunt Bertha and Doctor LeRoy were sitting on the couch. Instead of hostile looks I was greeted by smiling faces. I couldn't figure it out. And I'll be a yellow blackbird if Papa didn't take out his purse and remove a silver dollar and hold it out toward me.

"You did it, J.D.," Papa said.

I was so stunned I couldn't think straight. "Did what?" I asked.

"The spanking you gave Frankie made him cry," Papa said, "and that enabled him to let out all the grief and terror bottled up inside him. You broke his mental block and made him remember."

I took the dollar from Papa and sat down.

"Does he remember what happened in Red Rock Canyon?" I asked.

"I remember," Frankie said.

Mamma kissed Frankie on the top of the head. "He was hysterical for about half an hour," she said. "Just crying and screaming. And then he began to talk. He remembers everything now."

I was so curious I thought I would burst. "Will somebody please tell me how Frankie escaped from the landslide?" I pleaded.

Dr. LeRoy said, "Let him tell you himself, John. The more he talks about it the better."

Frankie slid off Mamma's lap and walked over and stood in front of me. "You spanked me, John," he said, "but I'll tell you anyway."

I watched his eyes, red from crying, grow wide and his lips begin to tremble.

"Papa said we were going to town for supplies," he said. "Mamma didn't want to go because it was raining. Papa said we had to go. In the canyon was a big rock on the road so the wagon couldn't pass. Papa got the crowbar from the wagon. Papa always took a crowbar to move the big rocks when we went to town. Papa started to move the big rock. My brother Willie and me were standing in the road watching. There was a noise like a big thunder. Willie grabbed my hand and we began running up the road. Willie looked back. He said the slide was below the wagon and he was going back to help Papa unhitch the team because they couldn't turn the wagon around on the road. Willie told me to keep running up the road until I couldn't run any more."

Frankie began to breathe heavily as he relived the terrible experience. "I kept running until I heard a big noise that hurt my ears," he continued, his face becoming very pale. "I stopped and turned around. Papa and Willie were unhitching the team and Mamma was waiting for them. Then the mountain fell down and they were all gone." Tears came into his eyes. "They are all deaded," he said softly.

I wasn't aware I was crying until Frankie reached up and brushed my cheek with his fingers and I felt a wetness there.

"Why are you crying, John?" he asked. "It is my Mamma and Papa and brother who are deaded and not yours."

"I just feel like crying," I said.

Papa said, "There is no doubt there were two slides, one below where they were and the bigger one right over them."

Dr. LeRoy cleared his throat. "I didn't want to alarm your father or mother, John," he said, "but it is fortunate Frankie is very young. An older person seeing such a terrible thing happen to their family might not ever have recovered."

I stood up. "I've got to go do my chores now," I said.

"Can I help?" Frankie asked.

I remembered Papa had often said that faith in the Lord, time, and keeping busy were the best medicine for grief.

"You bet you can," I said.

CHAPTER FIVE

Frankie Takes Over

I THOUGHT MY TROUBLES with Frankie were over now that he was over his mental block. I was as mistaken as a farmer trying to milk a bull. Now that Frankie was normal, he turned out to be a real take-over kid. I started teaching him how to play checkers after supper. At eight o'clock Mamma announced it was time for us to take our baths and go to bed. It has always been a tradition in our house that the youngest has to take his Saturday-night bath first.

"Time for your bath, Frankie," Mamma said.

He was sitting on the Oriental rug next to the fireplace with me. He folded his arms on his chest with a stubborn look on his face. "Make John go first," he said.

"You are the youngest," I said. "That means you go first."

"I ain't going to take a bath until you do," he said.

"Please humor him," Mamma said. "Maybe he just wants to make sure you have to take a bath, too. Little boys are funny that way."

"There isn't anything funny about making a nine-year-old take a bath before a four-year-old," I said.

Papa got into the argument. "Do as your mother says, J.D.," he said. "Just for tonight."

What could I do? It was an order. I was in the tub taking my bath when I heard a knock on the door.

"What now?" I hollered.

"Frankie wants to see you taking your bath," Mamma called through the door.

"Send him in," I shouted. "But tell him not to get too near the tub or I'll drown him." I didn't mean it, of course, but I was still smarting because I had to take my bath before a four-year-old.

Mamma opened the door. "Now stop making such a big fuss over this," she reprimanded me.

Frankie walked over and looked at me in the tub. He nodded his head and smiled.

"Are you satisfied I'm taking a bath and not just sailing a boat in here?" I asked.

"If I have to take a bath," he said, "I'm going to make sure you have to take a bath too."

Boy, oh, boy, here was a kid who hated to take a bath even more than I did. He left the bathroom with Mamma. I finished bathing and washed out the tub. I put on a clean nightgown and robe. Then I went into the parlor to say good night. I started to leave the room as Mamma took

Frankie by the hand and led him out of the parlor.

"Just a minute, J.D.," Papa said. "Frankie has been through a terrible experience. I want you to humor him and give in to him for as long as he is in this house. Is that understood?"

"Yes, Papa," I said.

I usually fell asleep right away after taking a bath. But I didn't that night. I heard somebody coming up the stairs. Then Mamma came into the bedroom holding Frankie in her arms. She pulled the beaded chain that turned on the ceiling light.

"Frankie wants to sleep with you instead of me," she said. "He has already said his prayers."

I got out of bed so Mamma could put Frankie on the inside next to the wall after she had kissed him good night. She waited until I got back in bed and then turned off the light.

"Good night, Frankie," I said after Mamma had left the room.

"This is my bed," Frankie said, instead of saying good night.

I sat up. "This was my bed before you were born," I said. "Now stop trying to be funny and go to sleep."

He sat up in bed and folded his arms on his chest. "You get out of my bed," he said.

I lay back down. "Stop being silly and go to sleep," I told him.

Then I felt his hands on my back. And I'm darned if he didn't try to roll me out of the bed. I was about to really tell him off when I remembered what Papa had told me. I got out of bed and turned on the light. There was another bed in the room, where Tom had slept before he went away to

71

school. But there weren't any sheets, blankets, and pillow-case on it. I put on my robe and went down to the parlor.

"Why did you leave Frankie alone?" Mamma demanded. "And why aren't you in bed?"

"Because he said it was his bed and told me to get out of it," I said. "Give me a couple of sheets and a blanket and pillowcase and I'll sleep in Tom's bed. Papa said I had to humor Frankie."

Papa had evidently told Mamma what he had told me. She got up and went to the linen closet. She came back with the bedclothes in her arms.

"Want me to make up the bed for you?" she asked.

"No, thanks," I said as I took the armful of bedclothes. "I can do it."

I went back up to my room. Frankie lay in my bed, smil-ing, as he watched me make up Tom's bed. He looked so darn smug about it that I decided to teach him a lesson. I turned out the light and stood by the window. He didn't say any-thing until I'd stood there for a couple of minutes.

"Whatcha doing, John?" he asked.

"There is a full moon tonight," I said, making my voice quiver a little.

"You sound scared," he said. "Why are you afraid of the full moon?"

"I'm not afraid for myself," I said, "because I'm too old for the ghost."

He sat up in bed. "What ghost?" he asked, and I knew from the sound of his voice that he was frightened.

"The ghost of Silverlode comes up from his grave every night there is a full moon," I said. "He goes from house to house in Adenville until he finds a little boy sleeping all alone. He takes the little boy back to his grave with him."

I paused dramatically. "And the little boy is never seen or heard from again."

Then I got into Tom's bed. I knew I'd thrown a good scare into Frankie because he was still sitting up in bed. I couldn't help laughing, smothering the sound in my pillow. It served him right for making me take a bath first and taking my bed.

"John," he said softly.

"Shut up and go to sleep," I said. "You got your bed all by yourself just like you wanted."

"You can sleep in my bed with me if you want," he said.

"I don't ever want to sleep in your bed," I said. "Go to sleep. Maybe the ghost won't come to our house tonight."

"But maybe he will," Frankie cried softly.

"I'll know in the morning," I said. "If you are missing, I'll know the ghost got you and took you back to his grave with him. I'm going to sleep now. Good night."

I pretended to fall asleep by snoring. I heard Frankie begin to whimper. I opened one eye. I could see him still sitting up in bed. There was enough moonlight streaming through the window for me to see tears toppling down both his cheeks. It wasn't funny any more. The little fellow was scared to death. I watched him get out of bed. He came over and stood by my bed. Then he climbed into bed with me and put his arms around me and snuggled up close.

"Please don't let the ghost get me, John," he cried.

I couldn't take it any longer. I put my arm around him and hugged him. Then I thought of the consequences of what I had done. If Frankie told Papa and Mamma they would take away my allowance for months.

"I won't let the ghost get you if you promise me something," I said.

73

"I promise," he said eagerly.

"The ghost can't get you unless you are sleeping alone," I said. "If you promise not to tell Papa and Mamma about the ghost, I'll let you sleep with me every time there is a full moon."

He hugged me tight. "I promise," he said.

Frankie went right to sleep but I didn't. My conscience was bothering me more than it had during my entire life. What I had done out of sheer spite was ten times worse than anything Frankie had ever done to me. Scaring a little kid was just about as low-down a trick as a fellow could pull. I asked God to please not let my little brain get any more crazy ideas like that.

The next day was Sunday and Mamma always let everybody sleep a little later. I didn't wake up until she came into the bedroom. She had an old suit of mine and some other clothing she had washed and pressed for Frankie.

"I see you changed your mind about sleeping alone," she said to Frankie as he sat up in bed.

He started to open his mouth and then looked at me. My future allowance for an entire year was in his hands. And the strange part about it was that I knew I deserved to lose it for telling him the ghost story.

"John and I will sleep in our bed from now on," he said to my great relief.

Mamma smiled. "That is good," she said. "It means less washing and ironing of sheets and pillowcases. Do you want me to help you wash and get dressed?"

"Frankie is big enough to wash and dress himself," I said. "Aren't you, Frankie?"

He looked as pleased as if I'd just given him a new rocking horse. "You bet, John," he said proudly.

It was raining when we got up and still raining when we all returned from the Community Church that morning. I knew it was raining too hard to go outside to play. I took Frankie up to my room. I thought I could keep him amused by showing him my box of treasures. What a big mistake that was. He watched me pull the box from under the bed and open it. I showed him my slingshot first. He took it in his hands and carefully examined it. Then he put it on the floor by his side.

"My slingshot," he said.

I picked up the slingshot. "I didn't give it to you," I said. "I'm just showing it to you."

He grabbed it out of my hands. "My slingshot," he said stubbornly.

I knew he couldn't use the slingshot because the rubber bands on it were too strong for a kid his age to pull back.

"I'll make a little slingshot for you," I said.

"I want this one," he said. "My slingshot or I'll tell."

I wasn't about to give up my slingshot, which was made from a perfect Y branch of a cherry tree, even though Papa had told me to humor Frankie and give in to him.

"You'll tell what?" I asked.

"About the ghost," he said.

"But you promised not to tell," I protested.

"I didn't promise not to tell Aunt Bertha," he said smugly.

Boy, or, boy, this kid was really something. I knew if he told Aunt Bertha that she would tell Papa and Mamma.

"Your slingshot," I said. What else could I do?

He laid it to one side. Then he reached into my box and took out my cap pistol. "My cap pistol," he said, putting it by the slingshot.

"Your cap pistol," I said. Boy, oh, boy, this little conniver made my brother Tom look like The Good Samaritan.

Frankie kept helping himself to my treasures until there was nothing left in the box but my bank.

"My bank," he said as he picked it up.

"Oh, no you don't," I said as I took it away from him. "You can tell Aunt Bertha. You can tell Mamma. You can tell Papa. You can tell the whole world but I'm not going to let you blackmail me out of my life savings. And after you tell them, I'm going to take back all those things."

He thought for a moment. "All right, John, you can keep your bank," he said as if he was doing me a big favor.

Then my little brain got a brilliant idea. "You've had your fun," I said. "Now give me everything back or you'll sleep alone the next full moon."

"No, I won't," he said. "I'll go sleep with your Mamma."

This kid had the answer for everything. He pointed at my box. "My box now," he said. "You don't need it any more."

"Take it," I said.

Then I got a chair and stood on it to put my bank on the top shelf in the clothes closet. I knew Frankie couldn't reach it there. And for all I knew this kid might turn out to be a safe-cracker as well as a blackmailer. My conscience wasn't bothering me any more for telling Frankie the ghost story. I had paid plenty for telling him a lie.

It had stopped raining by the time dinner was served. Frankie put away more than his share of the roast chicken with giblet gravy, chestnut dressing, mashed potatoes, and peas. He also ate a big piece of angel food cake with ice cream.

I changed into my play clothes after dinner, which we

always ate at one o'clock on Sundays. There were two things a kid could do and have a lot of fun after a rainstorm. He could go walking on stilts through rain puddles or go wading through them barefoot.

Mamma stopped me on my way through the kitchen. "Take Frankie with you," she said.

"He can't walk on stilts," I protested. "I'm going walking in the rain puddles."

"Not today you aren't," Mamma said. "I'll change him into some of your old clothes. You can take him for a ride in your wagon through the mud puddles and go barefoot yourself."

"Boy, oh, boy," I said with disgust, "it is getting to where I'm nothing but Frankie's slave around here."

"We don't know what your Uncle Mark is going to find at the Pennyworth farmhouse," Mamma said sharply. "Frankie may only be with us a few more days if your uncle locates some relatives. You will treat Frankie as your own little brother for as long as he is with us."

Mamma had spoiled my afternoon but had given me hope. Uncle Mark was sure to find Frankie had relatives. I was ready on the back porch when Mamma brought Frankie out. I had on knee pants and had my shoes and stockings off to wade barefooted. Mamma had dressed Frankie in some old jeans and shirt of mine.

I got my wagon off the porch. He climbed into it. I pulled him out of the backyard and down the alley to the street. I could see several kids wading through rain puddles on stilts or barefooted. Howard Kay and Jimmie Peterson were both barefooted. They came running through the rain puddles to meet me.

"Is that the kid?" Howard asked, pointing at Frankie.

I figured everybody in town knew about Frankie by now. "Yeah," I said. "His name is Frankie Pennyworth."

Jimmie hitched up his jeans. His mother always bought his clothing one size too big so he could wear clothes for two years. "What a funny name," he said.

Howard Kay laughed. "A penny's worth of what," he said.

Frankie looked at Jimmie. "Your pants are too big and you look funny," he said. Then he looked at Howard. "You've got a funny face," he said.

"Saucy little kid, ain't you?" Howard said.

Just then I saw Seth Smith go riding by on Tom's bike. He was deliberately riding through all the rain puddles he could. No kid who owned a bike would do a thing like that. He would know it would rot the tires and make the sprocket, chain, and spokes rusty.

"Is Sammy renting out Tom's bike on a day like this?" I asked, although I knew the answer.

"Yeah," Howard said. "I saw Danny Forester riding it through the deepest puddles he could find a while ago."

"I'll put a stop to that," I said. Boy, oh, boy, was I angry.

I pulled Frankie to the Smith's vacant lot. Sammy was there with his alarm clock. Five kids were waiting to pay for a ride. I let go of the handle of the wagon and walked up to Sammy.

"You can't rent Tom's bike when the streets are muddy and the kids ride it through puddles," I said. "You'll rot the tires and ruin the sprocket, chain, and spokes."

"What do I care?" Sammy asked with a shrug. "It ain't my bike."

"If it was your bike," I said, "I'll bet you wouldn't even use it yourself on a day like this."

"That is one bet you'd win," Sammy said. "But like I said, it ain't my bike."

"You are a no-good, yellow-bellied cheater," I said.

"Nobody calls me that and gets away with it," Sammy said, handing the alarm clock to Parley Benson. He drew a line in the muddy dirt with the toe of his shoe. "You ain't got your brother Tom here to protect you. Take it back or cross the line."

I knew Sammy was trying to get even with me for the times my brother had whipped him. He was more than a head taller than me and outweighed me plenty. I knew I didn't have a ghost of a chance of beating him. I knew if I crossed the line I'd end up with a bloody nose and a black eye. But I also knew I had to cross that line. For my money Sammy was a no-good, yellow-bellied cheater and I wasn't going to take it back. I took off my jacket and cap and handed them to Howard.

Parley Benson stepped between me and Sammy. "This ain't a fair fight," he said.

"Any fight is a fair fight if a boy steps across the line," Sammy said. "Tell him to take it back or cross the line."

I motioned for Parley to get out of the way. I doubled up my fists and put up my guard as I stepped across the line.

Sammy didn't even bother to take off his cap and jacket, knowing he could whip me easily. He threw a punch at me. I ducked. Then I began slamming away with both fists. I did get in a couple of good punches before Sammy landed a hay-maker on my left eye and knocked me down. He jumped on top of me and straddled my body, pinning me down. He scooped up a handful of mud. I knew he was going to make me take back what I'd said or eat it.

I heard Frankie yell, "You leave John alone!" Then

Frankie jumped on Sammy's back. He wrapped his arms around Sammy's neck. He got Sammy's right ear between his teeth and bit it. Sammy reached to try to pull Frankie off his back, but Frankie bit him on the hand so hard it made the hand bleed. Then he clamped his teeth on Sammy's ear again.

"Get this kid off me!" Sammy shouted.

None of the kids watching made a move.

"You let John alone or I'll bite your ear off!" Frankie yelled. Then he again clamped his teeth on Sammy's ear.

Sammy jumped to his feet, but Frankie still clung to his back. He tried to grab Frankie's arms. Frankie bit him so hard it made the ear bleed.

I was on my feet by this time. I stepped up to Sammy. He started to raise his hands but dropped them when Frankie bit his ear some more. I let Sammy have a haymaker on the nose so hard it made it bleed. I wanted to hit him some more but it didn't seem fair when he was afraid to hit back.

"Please get him off me," Sammy pleaded.

"Word of honor, you won't try to get even when I'm alone," I said.

"Word of honor," Sammy said quickly.

"Word of honor, no more renting Tom's bike when it rains," I said.

"Word of honor," Sammy cried. "Just get this kid off my back before he bites off my ear. I don't want to go around with just one ear."

Sammy was a bully and a slick one. But I knew if he ever broke his word of honor, no kid in town would have anything to do with him. I stepped behind him and put my hands under Frankie's armpits.

"You can let go now, Frankie," I said.

He let go with his teeth and arms. I lifted him down to

the ground. He walked in front of Sammy, who was holding a handkerchief to his ear. The handkerchief was red with blood. Blood was running from his nose. Frankie kicked him on the shins.

"Don't you dare hurt John again," Frankie said, as if he was twice as big as Sammy.

Sammy looked at Parley Benson. "Tell Seth to bring the bike to my house," he said. Then he started to run faster than I'd ever seen him run before.

I learned later that Dr. LeRoy had to take three stitches in Sammy's right ear. The big bully carried the scar for life.

Frankie climbed into the wagon. All the kids just stood there staring at him with their mouths open. It was as if all of them were suddenly paralyzed. I couldn't blame them for being stunned. Every one of them was afraid of Sammy Leeds, except maybe Parley Benson. I couldn't help feeling proud of Frankie as I pulled him in the wagon toward home. Maybe he was a take-over kid when it came to my possessions but he had just proved he liked me well enough to fight for me. And somehow that seemed to make everything even.

I put the wagon on the back porch. Frankie stood looking at it for a moment.

"My wagon," he said.

I was about to tell him the wagon was too big for him but I didn't. "Your wagon," I said.

I had a beaut of a black eye so I had to tell Mamma, Papa, and Aunt Bertha about the fight. Frankie helped me do my chores that afternoon. Uncle Mark came to the house while we were doing them. He had spent the night at the Pennyworth farmhouse. He was talking to Papa when Frankie and I entered the parlor.

Uncle Mark sure looked pleased that Frankie had got rid of the mental block. "Do you remember me?" he asked.

Frankie stared at him for a moment. "You're the man on the horse with the badge," he said.

"Right you are," Uncle Mark said, smiling. Then his face became serious. "Mr. Fitzgerald has told me about the accident. But I want you to tell me all about it, too."

Frankie told him about the same thing he had told me. When he finished, my uncle nodded his head and he looked at Papa.

"I think your deduction about there being two slides is correct," he said. He shook his head sadly. "They might have escaped if Mr. Pennyworth hadn't tried to save the horses."

"They are all deaded," Frankie said.

I wondered why he always said "deaded" instead of "dead." I also wondered why Mamma, who was in the parlor with Aunt Bertha at the time, didn't correct him. If I as much as said "ain't" she corrected me.

"Now, son," Uncle Mark said, tapping a tin box with a lock on it that he was holding on his knees, "I found the marriage license of your mother and father and the government homestead papers in this box at the farmhouse. But I couldn't find any letters from any relatives. Did your mother or father ever mention any relatives who are living?"

"They are all deaded," Frankie said.

Uncle Mark turned to Papa. "According to the marriage license the Pennyworths were married in Sedalia, Missouri. I'll send their marshal a telegram."

Mamma leaned forward in her chair. "What if you fail to find any relatives?" she asked.

"I'll get a court order and sell the farm at auction,"

Uncle Mark said. "I doubt if it will bring much now that the Red Rock Canyon road can't be used any more. Cathie will be back Thursday. We will talk about Frankie's future then."

I knew right then if Uncle Mark didn't find any relatives that he and my aunt Cathie wanted to adopt Frankie. They didn't have any children of their own. My aunt had given birth to a baby girl several years before but the baby had been born dead and my aunt had almost died. Dr. LeRoy had told her and Uncle Mark if they tried to have any more children Aunt Cathie might die.

The next morning I got up and dressed for school.

"Where are you going?" Frankie asked.

"I've got to go to school today," I said.

"Willie didn't have to go to school," he said. "Mamma and Papa taught Willie how to read and write."

"It is different when you live in a town," I said. "The only way a kid can miss one day of school is to have some contagious disease."

"Why don't you get one?" he asked.

"It wouldn't do any good," I said. "Then I'd just have to stay after school and do extra homework until I made up the time I lost ."

"I don't want you to go," he said.

"And I don't want to go, but I have to."

Frankie was waiting at the front gate for me when I came home for lunch. He took hold of my hand and held it tight as if he'd missed me. Papa arrived a few minutes later with news. But he didn't tell us until we were eating lunch.

Uncle Mark had dropped in at the *Advocate* office and told Papa he'd received a telegram from the marshal in Sedalia, Missouri. Frankie was right. His paternal grandparents

had died before his father left Missouri. His maternal grandparents had died after his mother left Missouri. His father
had a sister who had died when she was a child. His mother
had two brothers who had died during a small-pox epidemic.
After receiving the telegram, Uncle Mark had got a court
order from Judge Potter and the Pennyworth farm would be
sold at auction. My uncle had left town to arrange for the
auction and would return on Wednesday.

Uncle Mark did return on Wednesday. He had sold the
farm lock, stock, and barrel for five hundred dollars. The
money was given to Judge Potter to be put in trust at the
Adenville bank for Frankie.

Aunt Cathie arrived home on the afternoon train the
next day. She came to our house with Uncle Mark right after
supper that evening. I guess you would call my aunt beautiful. She has dark brown hair and eyes that seem always to
have a sparkle in them. Uncle Mark introduced her to
Frankie and he seemed fascinated by her.

"You're pretty," he said.

"Thank you, Frankie," she said as she sat down on the
couch beside her husband. "And you are a very handsome
young man."

That "young man" pleased him. I could see his chest
swell up. And I couldn't help feeling jealous. I knew it was
ridiculous to feel jealous of my own aunt but that is how I
felt.

Uncle Mark leaned forward. "Do you know what adoption is, Frankie?" he asked.

"I don't think so," Frankie said.

"When a boy's parents are dead," Uncle Mark said, "and
he has no living relatives to give him a home, a judge, like
Judge Potter, can sign papers letting somebody who isn't a

relative adopt the boy. My wife and I want to adopt you. That means when the judge signs the papers I'll legally become your father and Cathie your mother. We have no little boy of our own and would love to have you for our son. We promise to love you and take care of you just the same as if you were our own son. Do you understand?"

Frankie stared at Uncle Mark for a moment. "You mean you want to be my new papa and my new mamma?" he asked.

Aunt Cathie nodded her head. "Yes, dear, please," she said.

"And I would have to go live in your house instead of here?" Frankie asked.

"That is right," Uncle Mark said.

Mamma leaned forward and smiled at Frankie. "Mark and Cathie can't have any children unless they adopt them. They want to adopt you very much. You will make them happy and they will make you happy."

I could feel Frankie's hands on my knees begin to tremble.

"You don't ask me what I want," he cried as tears came into his eyes. "You only ask me what they want."

"But, Frankie . . ." Mamma started to say something, but Uncle Mark interrupted her.

"Let him talk, Tena," my uncle said. Then he looked at Frankie. "What do you want, son?"

"I want to stay here!" Frankie cried.

He broke away from me and ran over to Mamma, who picked him up and held him on her lap. He put his arms around her neck.

"I won't go!" he cried. "Why can't you be my new mamma and John's papa my new papa and John my new brother?"

Uncle Mark placed his hand over Aunt Cathie's hand. "I guess that settles it," he said and his voice was hoarse.

Aunt Cathie's eyes were blurred with tears as she nodded. "I know, dear," she said.

"I know how much this meant to you and to me," Uncle Mark said, "so we will do the next best thing. Sheriff Baker will be back Monday. We will go to the orphanage in Salt Lake City and adopt a boy."

Aunt Cathie's face brightened with a smile. "And a little girl," she said.

Then Uncle Mark smiled. "And a little girl," he said.

Frankie pulled his head back and stared into Mamma's face. "Does that mean you're going to adopt me?" he asked and seemed to be holding his breath waiting for her answer.

"Yes, dear," Mamma said as she kissed him on the cheek.

Uncle Mark turned to Papa. "I'll have Judge Potter draw up the adoption papers in the morning," he said. Then he smiled at Frankie. "Well, Frankie, at least I'll get to be your uncle and Cathie your aunt."

Frankie pointed to Aunt Bertha. "Aunt Bertha will be my aunt too," he said with a happy smile.

When I arrived home from school the next afternoon, Aunt Bertha told me that Papa, Mamma, and Frankie had gone to Judge Potter's chambers. I was too excited and curious to go out and play. I waited in the parlor for them. In a few minutes the front doorbell rang. I opened the door and saw Mr. Kramer.

"I stopped at your father's newspaper office but he wasn't there," he said. "Is he home?"

"No, sir," I said. "He is with Judge Potter and I don't know exactly when he will be back."

Alex Kramer took out a purse and removed a twenty-dollar gold piece, which he handed to me. "Please give this to your father for me and thank him for the loan. I am leaving town right away."

"You got Mr. Ferguson the team of mules," I said.

"Yes," Mr. Kramer said. "And he paid me a very handsome price for them."

"I tried your system but it didn't work," I said, because I thought he should know.

"Perhaps you don't have the knack for it," he said.

"That is what Papa said."

"Well, good-bye, John," he said. "And once again, please thank your father for the favor."

Papa, Mamma, and Frankie returned about fifteen minutes after Alex Kramer had left. They were all very happy.

"You are now my very own son," Mamma said, picking Frankie up in her arms and hugging him. "I promise that I will love you just as your own mother loved you."

Papa patted Frankie on the head. "And I promise I will love you just as your own father loved you," he said.

Papa then left for his newspaper office. Mamma went to change her clothes. I was alone with Frankie. I held out my hand.

"We are brothers now," I said as we shook hands. "Do you know what that means?"

He nodded. "You want back your wagon and the other things," he said.

"No," I said. "A deal is a deal. But you don't get anything else I own just by saying it is yours. The most important thing about being brothers is that when they share a secret, they don't tell anybody, not even their mother and father."

"You mean about the ghost," he said. "I wasn't really going to tell on you even if you didn't give me all those things. I don't tattle-tale on people I love."

I wasn't one for getting mushy but I couldn't help it. I picked him up and hugged him.

CHAPTER SIX

The Escape of Cal Roberts

I NEVER REALIZED UNTIL Frankie became my adopted brother how nice it was having a younger brother. I enjoyed teaching him how to play dominoes and checkers and other games. I liked reading to him. It was fun just to read aloud books like *Tom Sawyer* and *Huckleberry Finn.* I got a nice warm feeling inside making a slingshot, whistles from tree branches, and other things for him. And the way he looked up to me made me feel important. It was terrific knowing he would be waiting at the front gate for me when I came home from school, and would run to meet me as if I was the greatest fellow in the world. I think the bond between us was even greater than if he had been my real brother.

In the middle of November I got Tom's bike back from Sammy. It was a mess. The tires were worn down to where you could hardly see the treads. Both of them had been punctured several times. Sammy had fixed the punctures himself. We didn't have a bicycle shop in Adenville. There was a special needle that came with the tool case. Elastic bands were stretched on it and then dipped in a special glue. The needle and elastic bands were inserted in the hole in the tire. Then the needle was withdrawn, leaving the elastic bands with glue in the hole. Finally, matches were used to burn off the elastic bands and vulcanize the hole. The sprocket was in even worse condition. It slipped, and the brake was rusty and didn't work right. Mr. Harmon at the Z.C.M.I. stored looked it over and said it would be better to order a new sprocket. I was able to clean up the chain and spokes.

It was just a week after I got the bike back that Papa came home one evening looking worried. As usual, he postponed the bad news until after supper when we were all sitting in the parlor. Mamma could always tell when something was bothering Papa just as I could.

"What is the matter, dear?" she asked.

Papa exhaled some smoke from the cigar he was smoking. "Mark received a telegram this afternoon stating that Cal Roberts and five of his gang escaped from the penitentiary," Papa said solemnly. "They are believed to be heading this way."

"Oh dear God!" Mamma cried.

I didn't blame Mamma for being alarmed. Cal Roberts and his gang had terrorized southwestern Utah until they finally had been captured and convicted. They were cattle rustlers who stole cattle from big ranchers and drove them over the Nevada line to sell. Papa had often said the gang had

committed enough crimes, including murder, to hang all of them ten times. But the only witnesses they ever left behind were dead witnesses. They wouldn't have been arrested and convicted this time if the night herder they shot had been dead as they believed him to be.

Mr. James Bowman owned a big ranch about twenty miles from Adenville. All the ranchers employed night herders for several reasons. The night herders protected the steers, especially calves, from wolves and coyotes and mountain lions. They also played a harmonica or sang to the cattle if there was a storm to prevent the herd from stampeding. And they acted as lookouts for rustlers.

About a year before a night herder named Charlie Felkner had been riding night herd on the Bowman ranch. One of the Cal Roberts gang got close enough to shoot Felkner in the back with a rifle. The night herder fell from his horse. He was wounded and knew he couldn't fight off the gang by himself so he pretended he was dead. In the bright moonlight he recognized Cal Roberts. The rustlers cut out fifty head of prime beef and began driving the cattle toward the Nevada line.

The rustlers would have got away this time too if Felkner had been dead, because he wasn't due to be relieved by another night herder for four days. That would give the rustlers plenty of time to drive the stolen cattle over the Nevada line and sell them.

Felkner managed to climb on his horse after the rustlers had left and ride to the ranch house. Mr. Bowman got six of his cowboys and rode into Adenville about eleven o'clock that night. Uncle Mark swore them in as deputies and also deputized several other men.

The posse caught up with the rustlers the next morning. There was a gun battle during which one of the rustlers was killed and one deputy wounded. Cal Roberts and the other five of his gang surrendered, knowing they didn't have a chance against the posse. They were brought to Adenville for trial. They couldn't be charged with murder because they had only wounded the night herder and deputy. District Attorney Vickers decided to prosecute them for cattle-rustling. They were convicted by a jury and each of them sentenced to twenty years in the penitentiary.

Cal Roberts stood up in court after the sentence was pronounced. He swore he would break out of the penitentiary and get even with Judge Potter, District Attorney Vickers, and the foreman of the jury. Papa had been the foreman of the jury. That was why Mamma was so worried.

Aunt Bertha clasped her hands tightly in her lap. "Do you think he will try to keep that horrible threat he made in court?" she asked breathlessly.

Pappa knocked the ashes off his cigar into an ashtray. "It is quite possible," he said. "You can only hang a man once for murder, no matter how many people he kills. Roberts and his gang killed two prison guards in making their escape. However, I do believe Mark will have the situation well in hand if they do come here seeking revenge."

"Just what precautions is Mark taking?" Mamma asked.

Papa told us Uncle Mark was putting up wanted posters for the six men all over town. This would enable anybody who hadn't seen the gang at the trial to recognize them. Uncle Mark had also sworn in twenty deputies.

"Mark seems to think," Papa continued, "that if they are going to strike, they will do it at night. Roberts and his gang will realize that every man in town will be wearing a gun during the daytime."

"Just how would they strike at night?" Mamma asked.

"Mark has a theory and it seems like a good one," Papa said. "He believes the gang will sneak into town after midnight when the saloons and other businesses are closed. There are six of them. Mark believes two will go after Judge Potter, two after District Attorney Vickers, and the other two after me to make good Roberts' threat. Mark wanted to put the three of us in a room at the Sheepmen's Hotel where it would be easier to guard us. But we all refused to do it."

"Why?" Mamma asked. "It sounds like a very sensible thing to do."

"Because we had ample time to study the character of Cal Roberts during the trial," Papa said. "He is a very vain and vindictive man. His vanity will force him to try to carry out his threat. If he finds we are beyond his reach, he is vindictive enough to seek revenge upon our families. He would not hesitate to kill women and children." Papa paused for a moment. "But even if none of this were true, we are not the type of men who would let scum like Roberts drive us from our homes."

"Then Mark will protect our homes," Mamma said.

"He will place armed deputies on the back porch and the front porch of all three homes," Papa said. "There will also be an armed deputy across the street from each home. These deputies will be on duty from darkness to dawn. Mark and five deputies will sleep days and be on duty at the Marshal's office at night. There will also be armed deputies patrolling the streets both day and night. I agree with Mark that Roberts would be stupid to attempt anything during the daytime and that the gang will strike at night."

Frankie, who had been sitting on the floor with me, got up and walked over to Mamma. "I don't want the bad mans to hurt my new papa," he cried.

Mamma was so worried she didn't bother to correct his grammar as she picked him up and hugged him. "Don't you worry about it, dear," she said. "Your uncle Mark will take care that the bad men don't hurt anybody."

Frankie and I went to bed after Papa said the outlaws couldn't possibly reach Adenville that night. Frankie knelt to pray.

"Please God," he prayed, "don't let the bad mans hurt my mamma and papa and brother and Aunt Bertha. If the bad mans must hurt somebody, let it be me. Amen."

I held Frankie in my arms that night until he fell asleep. I couldn't help but be moved at his love and goodness.

The next morning after breakfast I watched Papa strap on his holster with his revolver before leaving for the *Advocate* office. I thought for sure there wouldn't be any school until the outlaws were captured. But I was as wrong as a fish who decides he can live out of water.

Adenville was an armed camp for the next two days and nights. Three deputies were guarding our house from the time it got dark until daylight. Ken Smith was on our front porch with a shotgun and pistol. Don Huddle was on our back porch, also armed with a shotgun and pistol. And Ben Daniels was across the street from our house armed with a rifle and pistol. But nothing happened until the third night.

Uncle Mark was right about the gang striking at night. But he was wrong about how they would do it. They didn't sneak into town. All six of them rode into town about two o'clock in the morning. They rode at a gallop right down

Main Street shooting out windows in the Marshal's office and places of business. They exchanged shots with deputies on patrol, but nobody was hit. It is almost impossible to hit a man hunched over in the saddle on a galloping horse. And it is also almost impossible for the man on the horse to hit anything while riding at a gallop.

The gang stopped when they reached the end of Main Street on the east side of town. They got off their horses and took cover by the livery stable and blacksmith shop. They had Main Street on the east side covered this way. A gun battle began to rage between the deputies and outlaws.

The deputies guarding the three homes heard the shooting. They believed the outlaws were cornered, so they left their posts. Uncle Mark and the five deputies came out of his office right after the shooting started. They mounted their horses and rode down to the other side of the railroad tracks. The outlaws were shooting blindly down the street. Deputies were shooting back from behind empty beer kegs, a water trough, and from doorways of buildings.

Then Uncle Mark saw the deputies who were supposed to be guarding the three homes come running down Main Street. That was when Uncle Mark proved he was a very smart law officer. He figured this shooting was just a diversion to draw the deputies away from the three homes. He guessed that Cal Roberts had left part of his gang at the end of Main Street, while he and the rest of his gang were circling around the outskirts of town and going back to the west side. Uncle Mark had a terrible decision to make in a second. But he knew as a lawman his first duty was to protect Judge Potter. He ordered two deputies named Johnson and Stevens to follow him. They rode at a gallop to the Judge's house.

Judge Potter and his wife had been awakened by the

sound of gunfire. They got out of bed, put on their robes, and went into the parlor. Judge Potter called to the deputy who was supposed to be guarding the front porch. He received no answer. Then he went to the back porch and discovered that deputy also gone. He armed himself with a rifle and sat in the parlor with his wife. He was watching out the front window when he saw two men ride up and dismount in front of his house. They kept their heads down and it was too dark for the Judge to recognize them. They walked to the front porch. The two men were Cal Roberts and Jack Austin.

"Are you all right, Judge?" Austin called through the front door. "Mark Trainor sent us to check on you. The gang is bottled up on the east side of town."

Judge Potter didn't recognize the voice but assumed my uncle had sent two deputies after discovering the others had left the Judge's home unprotected. He opened the door. Austin grabbed the rifle away from him and used the butt of it to knock Mrs. Potter unconscious.

"Get the rope," Cal Roberts said, holding a pistol against the Judge's head. "We don't want any shootin' to attract attention."

Austin ran to his horse and came back with a rope. The outlaws had planned carefully. The rope had a hangman's noose on the end of it. He put the noose around Judge Potter's neck and tightened it.

"Goin' to hang you, Judge," Roberts said, "just like you would like to hang me. Goin' to hang you on that tree in front of your house. Then I'll get them other two and hang them too."

Uncle Mark saw the two horses in front of the Judge's house and he and his deputies dismounted a block away.

Then all three of them ran toward the house. The outlaws were about to hang Judge Potter when Uncle Mark got within revolver range. He shouted for the outlaws to surrender. Austin ran for his horse. Uncle Mark shot and killed him.

Using the Judge as a shield, Cal Roberts fired three shots. One bullet hit Deputy Johnson, who fell to the ground. Uncle Mark and Deputy Stevens were afraid to shoot back for fear of hitting the Judge. Then Roberts threw the Judge to the ground and fired a shot at him before running for the corner of the house. Uncle Mark and Deputy Stevens opened fire. Uncle Mark said later he believed one of their bullets had hit the outlaw.

My uncle had told me one time that any outlaw who belonged to a gang of bandits was a coward at heart. He said the only outlaws with real courage were the ones who worked alone. Cal Roberts proved my uncle to be right that night. He must have become panic-stricken after Austin was killed. If he'd had real courage and used his head, he would have put his pistol to Judge Potter's head and threatened to kill him if Uncle Mark didn't let him escape. My uncle admitted he would have done just that to save the Judge's life. But Cal Roberts, facing danger all by himself, ran instead.

Uncle Mark and Deputy Stevens ran around the house after Roberts. They searched the backyard and alley without finding the outlaw. Cal Roberts had escaped on foot. Uncle Mark ordered Deputy Stevens to get the wounded Judge and deputy into the house and send for Dr. LeRoy. Then he mounted his horse. Once again he was faced with a terrible decision. Cal Roberts alone might be a coward but he still might be vain enough to try to kill the District Attorney or my father. Uncle Mark rode to the home of the District Attorney because he knew that was where his sworn duty as a lawman belonged first.

When the shooting first started, it woke Frankie and me. I knew what it was all about right away. We put on our robes and ran downstairs. The noise of gunfire had awakened Papa, Mamma, and Aunt Bertha, who were in the parlor with robes thrown over their nightgowns.

"It sounds as if they are making a fight of it on the east side of town," Papa said. "As a journalist I should be there."

Papa went into his bedroom and I'll bet he never got dressed so quickly in his life.

"I'll check with Ken and Don before I leave," he said.

When Papa went to the front porch and then the back porch and discovered both deputies missing, he went to the gun rack and got a double-barreled twelve-gauge shotgun. He put shells in it and handed it to Mamma.

"Ken and Don must have heard the shooting on the east side and gone there," Papa said. "But we can't afford to take any chances. You take the front porch, Tena, and shoot any man coming into the front yard who doesn't identify himself. I'll get the rifle and take the back porch. Bertha, you take the boys and go down into the cellar. And keep quiet no matter what you hear up here. Let us move quickly now."

I started to protest that I was big enough to use a rifle but didn't get a chance. Aunt Bertha grabbed Frankie and me by the hands and ran with us into the dark, cold cellar.

I could hear the sound of pistol shots, rifle shots, and shotguns but none near enough to be Papa or Mamma shooting. It seemed like we were in the cellar a long time before I heard Brownie barking. It was an alarm bark.

"There is somebody out in back," I told Aunt Bertha. "I must warn Papa."

I knew she'd try to stop me so I ducked around her and ran up to the kitchen. I opened the back door.

"There is somebody out there, Papa," I called to him. "Brownie wouldn't bark that way if there wasn't."

"You get back in the cellar and stay there," he ordered me. "It is just the noise of the shooting that is making your dog bark."

Papa could be right. On the Fourth of July when the kids were setting off firecrackers, all the dogs in town barked like crazy. When I returned to the cellar, Frankie found my hand in the darkness and held it tight.

"Are the bad mans going to kill Mamma and Papa?" he asked and it sounded as if he was crying.

"Heck, no," I said. "If Cal Roberts or any of his gang come around here they will get their heads shot off. Mamma can handle a gun as well as any man and Papa is a crack shot."

We remained in the cellar for about half an hour before we heard doors opening and footsteps upstairs. Then Mamma called to us that we could come up.

Uncle Mark was with Papa in the parlor and he looked both worried and angry. "I'm putting two men in back and two in front," he said. "And this time I'm giving them strict orders not to leave. I've got men covering the Judge's and District Attorney's homes."

"Then it is all right if I go with you," Papa said.

"Your family will be safe enough now," Uncle Mark said. "I believe Cal Roberts left four men to create a diversion while he and Austin carried out the murders. Those four men can hold off an army coming down Main Street. And

101

there is no way to get at them from the rear because it is open country. Anyone trying it would make a wide open target and be cut down. The plan as I see it was for Roberts and Austin to commit the murders and then circle the town and join up with the others. They would then all ride out to the east. I'd need a troop of cavalry to stop them, especially at night."

"The men left to create the diversion will know something is wrong when Roberts and Austin don't return," Papa said.

Uncle Mark's face became thoughtful for a moment. "You've given me an idea," he said. "If I ride Roberts' pinto horse and Hal Benson rides Austin's gray horse the outlaws will recognize the horses. Hal can wear the hat and jacket Austin had on when killed. I've got a black hat and buckskin jacket at home like Roberts was wearing. If Hal and I keep our heads down, the outlaws will think we are Roberts and Austin. This will give us a chance to take them from the rear and catch them in a cross fire."

"What if Roberts has circled the town on foot and joined his gang?" Papa asked. "You and Hal are certain to be killed."

"It is a risk we will have to take," Uncle Mark said, "but a small risk. If Roberts did join his gang, he would leave with them immediately, stealing a horse from the livery stable. There would be no sense in remaining after his plan failed."

Papa left the house with Uncle Mark. Mamma made Frankie and me go to bed. I could still hear shooting when I fell asleep.

The next morning Frankie and I put on our robes and ran downstairs to the kitchen. Papa was drinking coffee. He looked tired, as if he's been up all night.

"What happened?" I shouted.

"Your Uncle Mark's plan worked," Papa said. "Three of the outlaws are dead and one seriously wounded. But Cal Roberts escaped."

I felt the hair on my head get stiff as a hairbrush. "That means he will organize another gang and come back again," I said.

"We don't know if he managed to steal a horse last night and leave town or not," Papa said. "We will know in a few hours."

"How?" I asked.

"Mark and the deputies are checking everybody in town who owns horses," Papa answered.

"What about Dusty?" I asked, remembering Brownie's alarm bark of the night before.

"I've looked in the barn," Papa said. "Dusty and our team are there."

"What if no horse is found missing?" I asked.

"It could mean any one of several things," Papa said. "Cal Roberts knows this country well. He might have made it on foot to a nearby farm or ranch and stolen a horse last night. He might have made it on foot out of town and stolen a horse from some lone rider coming into town. However, there is also the possibility that Cal Roberts might still be hiding out right in town. Mark and the deputies will search every barn and shack that a man might possibly use for a hide-out. If Cal Roberts isn't located in Adenville, the search will continue in the ghost town of Silverlode. A man could easily hide in all those old mine tunnels."

"Boy, oh, boy," I said. "I'm glad today is Saturday and no school. I'd hate to miss out on all the excitement. The first thing I want to see is where the desperadoes met their death at the livery stable and blacksmith shop."

"I'm afraid you are due for a disappointment," Papa said. "Your Uncle Mark has given orders that all persons under sixteen years of age are to remain in their own homes until the search is over. He doesn't want to have a couple hundred kids under foot during the search."

Papa was sure right. I'd never been so disappointed in my life.

Mamma was helping Aunt Bertha get breakfast ready. "You and Frankie wash up and get dressed now," she said.

The deputies guarding our house had left by the time Frankie and I finished eating breakfast. I did the morning chores with Frankie helping me. Every time I went into the barn, Brownie began barking his alarm bark. I figured he was still just excited from hearing all the shooting the night before. I couldn't leave our backyard, so I played with Frankie and Brownie and Prince until Mamma called that lunch was ready.

Papa told us during lunch that nobody in Adenville was missing a horse. Uncle Mark and a hundred men had begun searching every barn and shack in town. They had started on the east side of town and were working their way westward. After lunch Papa went back to the *Advocate* office to begin setting type for the news story about the Cal Roberts gang so it would be ready for Tuesday's weekly edition of the newspaper.

I went into our backyard with Frankie. I was surprised to see Howard Kay come down the alley and into our backyard.

"Weren't you told to stay home?" I asked.

"Sure," he said as he sat down beside me on the back porch steps. "But Ma is talking to Mrs. Smith over the back fence and they will be jawing for at least an hour. I knew that with your uncle being the marshal you'd know all about what happened last night."

It turned out that Howard didn't know beans about what had happened. I knew a lot of things he didn't know. I got so interested in telling him all about it that I didn't miss Frankie until Howard left about an hour later. I went looking for Frankie. He wasn't in the woodshed or icehouse or corral. Brownie was sitting by the barn door. When he began barking, I knew Frankie must be in the barn.

The first thing I noticed when I entered the barn was that the rope ladder had been pulled up into the loft.

"I know you are up there, Frankie," I called. "Throw down the ladder so I can come up."

The rope ladder came tumbling down. I climbed up, telling myself I had a right to be angry with Frankie. He was too little to be climbing up and down the rope ladder. If he had hurt himself it would be my fault for not keeping an eye on him. I forgot all about it when my head came up to where I could see into the loft. I became so frightened I almost lost my hold and fell.

Frankie was in the loft, all right, but not alone. He had a gag in his mouth made from a red bandana handkerchief. His hands were tied behind his back and his legs were trussed up with some pieces of rope Tom had left in the loft.

A man with a blond mustache and a scar on his cheek was holding a bowie knife about an inch from Frankie's throat. The left shoulder of his shirt and buckskin jacket were red with blood. His right pant leg was torn and bloody. I knew I was looking at Cal Roberts.

"Just keep comin', boy," he said, "unless you want me to slit this kid's throat."

105

CHAPTER SEVEN

Hostage

I CLIMBED INTO THE LOFT. My knees were so wobbly I couldn't stand up. I just remained on all fours staring at the outlaw.

"Know who I am, boy?" he asked as he put the bowie knife back in a scabbard on his belt.

"You are Cal Roberts," I said. "The man who swore he would kill my father."

"I came here fixin' to do just that last night while the Marshal was busy at the Judge's house," Roberts said. "But I saw the shine of a rifle barrel on your back porch, and I reckoned as how the deputy guardin' your house hadn't been fooled by the ruckus my boys were makin' on the other side of town. So I figured I'd steal a horse, but that damn dog bit my leg when I tried. I knew if I shot the dog it would attract the attention of the deputy."

I knew Cal Roberts had seen Papa on the back porch but hadn't recognized him in the darkness.

"My father was only doing his duty as a citizen serving on the jury," I said. "Why do you want to kill him for that?"

"If I just wanted to kill your pa," he said, "I could have killed him this morning when he came into the barn. But I knew the sound of the shot would attract attention and I'd never make it out of town. Anyway, when I saw this rope ladder last night it gave me an idea. I knew kids must use it and it was a good way for me to get a hostage."

"Please let Frankie go and make me your hostage," I pleaded.

"Nope," he said. "I need an older kid like you to take messages for me. Now you tell your pa and the Marshal I ain't makin' the same mistake I made with the Judge. I'm holdin' this kid as a hostage and if they try to flush me out of this barn I'll kill the kid first. You got that, boy?"

"Yes, sir," I answered.

"Next you tell them how I'm goin' to leave town," the outlaw said. "I'm ridin' out of here on that mustang you've got. And I'm goin' to be holdin' this kid on the saddle in front of me. And I'll be holding my cocked .45 against the back of this kid's head. I've got a hair trigger on my gun. Even if somebody shot me in the back or head, the hair trigger would blow this kid's brains out. The Marshal knows that is what would happen. You got that, boy?"

"Yes, sir," I said weakly, feeling a cold sweat break out all over my body. Papa was right. Cal Roberts was a low-down enough skunk to kill a little kid.

"The first thing I want is a doc to fix this arm," the outlaw said. "I got winged at the Judge's house last night. Then I want some vittles to eat and water to drink. And if anybody but you and the doc come into this barn, I'll shoot them first and then the kid. And you tell your pa that seein' as how I ain't goin' to kill him, I want one thousand dollars."

"But the bank is closed," I protested.

"Let them open it," he said.

"They can't open the vault until Monday morning," I said. "Mr. Whitlock put a time lock on it after the bank was robbed."

"That will give my shoulder an extra day to heal," Cal Roberts said. "I ain't in no hurry now I've got myself a hostage."

Just then we heard several dogs barking and the sound of men's voices.

"What's goin' on?" Roberts demanded.

"They are searching all the buildings in town looking for you," I answered.

Roberts removed his bowie knife from the scabbard and held it an inch from Frankie's throat. "You know what to tell them when they come in here," he said.

I put my head over the side of the loft. In a few minutes Jerry Stout came into the barn carrying a shotgun, and right behind him was Don Huddle with a rifle.

"There is nobody up here but me," I shouted.

They looked up at me.

"All right, John," Mr. Stout said.

I watched them look in the manger and behind bales of hay and every place a man might hide.

"I think this is a waste of time," Mr. Stout said. "Cal Roberts is long gone from this town."

"Only one way to make sure," Mr. Huddle said, "and that is to do exactly what we are doing."

Then the two men left the barn.

Roberts put his bowie knife back. "Get goin', boy," he ordered. "The doc first and then something to eat and drink. And if anything goes wrong, this kid gets his throat cut."

I looked at Frankie. I knew he'd been crying because his eyes were all red. But he hadn't cried one tear since I came into the loft.

"Don't worry, Frankie," I said. "Papa and Mamma aren't going to let anything happen to you." Then I turned to the outlaw. "Can't you take the gag out of his mouth for a while?" I asked.

"Maybe later," he said. "I put it in not only to shut him up but to stop him from bitin' me."

My legs were trembling as I climbed down the ladder. I held back the tears until I was out of the barn. I couldn't help feeling it was all my fault. If I'd been watching Frankie instead of talking to Howard Kay, he would never have climbed up to the loft by himself. Brownie was waiting for me. I patted him on the head. If only Papa had listened to me when I told him my dog was giving an alarm bark. If. If. If. All the ifs in the world couldn't change things now. I ran to the house and into the kitchen. Mamma and Aunt Bertha were baking pies. Mamma wiped her hands on her apron.

"What is the matter, John D.?" she cried.

"Get Papa and Uncle Mark and Dr. LeRoy quick!" I said. "But don't tell anybody else. Cal Roberts is hiding in the loft in our barn. He is holding Frankie as a hostage and will kill him if we don't do as he says."

Mamma reacted quickly, as she always did in a crisis. She ran to the telephone. Aunt Bertha staggered to a chair

109

and sat down. She didn't say anything. She just sat there, crying softly.

It seemed like hours but could only have been about fifteen or twenty minutes before Papa arrived with Uncle Mark and Dr. LeRoy. We were waiting for them in the parlor.

"What is it, Tena?" Papa asked. "You said it was urgent and to bring Mark and the doctor."

"I didn't want to tell you over the phone because the operator usually listens in," Mamma said. "Cal Roberts is in our barn and he's holding Frankie as a hostage. John D., tell them all you know."

I told them what I thought was everything. But when Uncle Mark began questioning me, I remembered several things I hadn't told them. Their faces were all grim when I finished.

Papa sat down in his rocking chair. "We must do exactly what Cal Roberts says."

"For the time being, at least," Uncle Mark said.

Dr. LeRoy was still standing, his doctor's bag in his hand. "Better take me to the barn now, John," he said.

I looked at Mamma. "You had better fix him something to eat right away," I said.

"I'll have it ready by the time you return," Mamma said.

I took Dr. LeRoy to the barn. The outlaw was leaning over the edge of the loft with his revolver pointing down at us as we entered. I told him I'd brought the doctor. Roberts threw down the rope ladder. Dr. LeRoy and I climbed up to the loft. The outlaw had taken off his jacket and shirt and had his underwear rolled down to his waist. I could see blood oozing from a wound on his arm just below the shoulder. He held his revolver against Frankie's ear.

110

"Fix it up, Doc," Roberts said. "And fix it good and tight so it can stand some hard ridin'."

Dr. LeRoy knelt down and examined the wound. "The bullet missed the bone," he said. "It is just a flesh wound. Nothing serious, I'm afraid."

"You say it like you wish it was serious," Roberts said.

"I was hoping it might be so serious you couldn't get very far on a horse without bleeding to death," Dr. LeRoy said.

"Stop jawing and get on with it," Roberts ordered.

Dr. LeRoy cleansed the wound and put some kind of salve and powder on it before he bandaged it up tight. Then he cleansed and bandaged the dog bite on the outlaw's leg.

"That will hold you until you get to wherever you are going," Dr. LeRoy said.

Roberts grinned. "That means the Marshal is seein' things my way," he said.

"If he wasn't," Dr. LeRoy said, "I wouldn't be here."

"How come the Marshal ain't out with a posse lookin' for my four boys?" Roberts asked.

"They are all dead," Dr. LeRoy said. "The last one died from his wounds about two hours ago."

Roberts shrugged. "I can always get myself another gang," he said. "But I don't get it. How come they didn't make a break for it when Austin and I didn't show up?"

"Because my Uncle Mark outsmarted them," I said.

"Always heard he was a right smart marshal," Roberts said. "But there just ain't no way he could stop them goin' east over that flat country at night."

"My uncle and Mr. Benson impersonated you and Jack Austin on your horses to get close enough to catch the outlaws in a cross fire," I said.

112

"Seems like a low-down trick for a marshal to pull," Roberts complained, to my astonishment.

I was about to say that holding a little kid as a hostage was about as low-down a trick as a man could play. But Dr. LeRoy closed his bag and said he was ready to leave.

"Well, at least I got the Judge," Roberts said.

Dr. LeRoy shook his head. "The bullet you fired at Judge Potter hit him in the leg," he said. "He is going to be all right."

"Damn," Roberts said.

I pointed at Frankie. "Can I take the gag out of his mouth, Mr. Roberts?" I asked.

"Only if he promises not to bite me," the outlaw said. "But I'm leavin' him tied up. He is the bitin'est, fightin'est, and kickin'est kid I ever saw."

I removed the gag from Frankie's mouth. He spit a couple of times.

"I asked God to let the bad mans get me and He did," Frankie said.

"Don't you worry," I said. "Papa and Mamma and Uncle Mark are going to do what Mr. Roberts wants and you'll be all right."

"Get me that grub now," Roberts ordered.

I followed Dr. LeRoy down the rope ladder and into the house. He went into the parlor to talk to Papa and Uncle Mark. Mamma had our wicker picnic basket ready for me.

"Tell Mr. Roberts there are ham and cold roast beef sandwiches and some pie and apples," Mamma said. "And tell him I will cook fried chicken or anything else he may want for supper. And I put a jug of milk and some cookies in for Frankie."

I carried the wicker basket to the barn. It had handles

that came up over the top. I hooked the handles inside my elbow. It was awkward but I managed to climb up to the loft with it.

Roberts grabbed the jug of water out of the basket first and drank a lot of it. Then he began eating a sandwich.

"There's a jug of milk and some cookies for Frankie," I said. "Can I give them to him?"

"I ain't untyin' the little wildcat," Roberts said. "Feed him yourself."

"I ain't hungry, John," Frankie said.

"But you always have milk and cookies this time every day," I said.

"I know," he said, "but I don't want any today."

It didn't hit me until then that although he didn't show it on the outside Frankie was so frightened inside that he couldn't eat anything.

"I know you are scared," I said, "but please at least drink the milk."

"All right," he said.

I got him to drink about half the milk and that was all.

Roberts ate all the sandwiches and the piece of pie and apples and even the cookies I'd brought for Frankie.

"My mother wants to know what you want for supper," I said. "She said she'd cook fried chicken or anything you wanted."

"Tell your ma fried chicken will do fine," he said. "And I'll want some hot coffee in a jug. And as long as I'm stayin' here tonight, I'll need a couple of blankets."

"When will you let Frankie go?" I asked

"I'm thinkin' about that," he said. "Ain't no hurry. Let you and your pa and the Marshal know my plans tomorrow."

114

"I've got to do my chores now," I said. "That means I have to take the mustang out to the corral to water him."

"I know you'll bring him back," Roberts said. "Just as I know everything is goin' my way. Gettin' me a hostage was the best idea I ever had."

After I'd finished all my chores I found Papa still talking to Uncle Mark in the parlor. Dr. LeRoy had left.

"Sit down, J.D.," Papa said. "There are some questions your uncle wants to ask you."

I sat down. "What questions?" I asked.

"Is there any way to get up to that loft except by the rope ladder?" Uncle Mark asked.

"No," I answered.

"Then is there any way to get up even with the rafters on the other side of the barn without using a ladder?" Uncle Mark asked.

"No," I answered. "Even if you stood on the stalls or the bales of hay you'd still be about twenty feet from the rafters. Why?"

"I am trying to figure out a way of getting up high enough in the barn tonight so I can shoot into the loft when it gets daylight," he said.

"Even if you could get up high enough, which you can't," I said, "the barn doors squeak like the devil and he would hear you when you opened them."

Papa shook his head. "There is absolutely no way to kill or capture Cal Roberts without endangering Frankie's life," he said. "That boy's life is as precious to me and Tena as the life of one of our own sons. I am going to insist that you do exactly what Cal Roberts demands."

"There is something wrong about all this," Uncle Mark

said. "I don't mean it is wrong to let Cal Roberts go scot-free to save Frankie's life. I mean there is something in the back of my mind that keeps telling me it just isn't that simple."

"This I know," Papa said. "You must let the search for Cal Roberts continue, including the ghost town of Silverlode. That will convince people the outlaw hasn't been found. If word gets out that Cal Roberts is in our barn, everybody in town will come here. And you can't control a mob like that. Some hotheads might get the idea of rushing the barn or setting it on fire to smoke Roberts out. Either way it would mean death for Frankie. We know Dr. LeRoy will keep it confidential. I will have to tell Mr. Whitlock at the bank Monday why I want to mortgage my home for a thousand dollars. But we can trust him. That leaves just you, Mark. I want your word of honor you will not mention this to anybody."

"That goes without saying," Uncle Mark said, as if irritated. "I'll let the search continue."

"What if some kids come over to play?" I asked. "We often play in our barn on Sunday afternoons, especially if it is raining."

"That is a good point, John," my uncle said. "I'll confine everybody under sixteen years of age to their own homes until this thing is over."

I took Cal Roberts and Frankie the fried chicken supper before we ate our own meal in the house. Frankie liked fried chicken just about better than anything. But I had a hard time making him eat just one wing and half a slice of bread.

"My stomach is all hard and won't eat," he told me.

116

I knew what he meant. The poor little fellow was all tied up in knots inside although he was acting brave in front of me.

I took the dirty dishes and picnic basket back to the house. Mamma had blankets and a couple of pillows ready for me. I made two trips up the rope ladder to get them to the loft. I asked Roberts if there was anything else he wanted.

"Tell your ma I want some ham and beans and biscuits and coffee for breakfast," he said. "And shut the barn doors when you leave. I gotta get some sleep."

I put a pillow under Frankie's head and covered him with a blanket. I knew how uncomfortable it must be for him with his hands tied behind his back and his legs tied together. But he hadn't complained one time.

"Good-bye, John," he said.

"Not good-bye, just good night," I said. "I'll see you in the morning."

"See you in the morning," he said.

Even Cal Roberts had to admire Frankie's courage. "He's a right spunky little devil," the outlaw said.

It was a very sad supper that evening. Nobody spoke except to have something passed to them. It was the same later as we sat in the parlor. Mamma kept dabbing her eyes with a handkerchief. Papa kept clearing his throat but not saying a word. Aunt Bertha let out a soft moan every once in a while. I had never felt so sad and lonely in my life. I was so used to having Frankie around, it was as if a part of me had died.

It was even worse after I'd taken my bath and went to bed. I thought of me sleeping in a nice soft bed while poor

117

Frankie was sleeping on hard boards. I got up and slept on the floor. It was as close as I could come to sharing Frankie's discomfort.

The next morning I took Cal Roberts and Frankie their breakfast.

"Good morning, John," Frankie said. "Are Papa and Mamma and Aunt Bertha all right?" His eyes were red from crying but he even smiled at me.

"They are fine," I said, "but worried because you won't eat anything."

"I don't want them to worry," he said. "So I'll make myself eat."

Roberts let me untie Frankie's hands so he could eat. But he tied them back up after the boy had finished.

"Reckon you've got your chores to do now," Roberts said. "But before you start, get a notebook and pencil and come back up here."

I took the picnic basket and dirty dishes back to the kitchen. I told Mamma that Frankie had finally managed to eat a meal. I got a school notebook and pencil and went back up to the loft.

"I've got it all figured out now," Roberts said. "But I don't want any slip-ups. Write down what I say. First I want the Marshal to give me a twenty-four-hour headstart. I keep the kid with me for twenty-four hours. Any sign anybody is followin' me and I kill the kid. Got that?"

I wrote down the demand and then nodded my head.

"Next, I want two saddlebags with enough beef jerky, hardtack, beans, and coffee to last for a week," Roberts said.

I wrote it down.

"Next, I want four big canteens filled with water," he

118

said. "And no tricks. I'm goin' to taste that water and so are you."

I wrote that down.

"You bring the saddlebags and canteens of water up here today," the outlaw said. "Tomorrow morning when your pa is gettin' the money from the bank, you saddle up the mustang and have him ready to go. Then you meet your pa and bring the money to me. Got that?"

I wrote it all down.

"As soon as I get the thousand dollars," Roberts said, "I'm ridin' outa here with the kid. And I'm ridin' right down Main Street with my cocked pistol against the back of the kid's head. Maybe I didn't get to kill the Judge and the District Attorney and your pa but I want everybody in town to see Cal Roberts put one over on the Marshal and the people in this town."

"You are a fool," I said without thinking.

He slapped me so hard on the side of the head it almost knocked me off the loft. "Nobody, includin' a kid, calls Cal Roberts a fool," he said.

"What I meant to say," I apologized, "was that it would be a lot safer for you at night. Nobody cares what happens to Frankie except Papa, Mamma, Aunt Bertha, Uncle Mark, Aunt Cathie, and me. Uncle Mark can't prevent somebody from taking a shot at you riding down Main Street in broad daylight. He can't stop men from organizing a posse and taking out after you if everybody in town sees you leave. If you wait until tomorrow night to leave nobody will know you were in our barn until twenty-four hours later."

"The Marshal put you up to sayin' that," the outlaw said, to my surprise. "He knows if I left at night, I couldn't see if there was a posse on my tail or not. He knows if I left at night, I'd leave myself wide open to be bushwhacked in the darkness. You tell the Marshal I'm leavin' my way tomorrow mornin' just like I planned. If somebody takes a shot at me, the kid will die. If I see a posse on my tail, the kid will die."

"When will you let Frankie go?" I asked.

"Not until I'm sure the Marshal has kept his word and given me a twenty-four-hour headstart," he answered.

"How will we know where to find Frankie?" I asked.

Roberts hesitated for almost a minute and then grinned. "I'll leave him in some town I'm passin' through," he said.

CHAPTER EIGHT

My Little Brain
Against Cal Roberts

I RETURNED TO THE HOUSE. I gave Papa the notebook with Cal Roberts' demands. Papa read them aloud.

"We might as well get started meeting these demands," Papa said. "With Mark confining everybody under sixteen to their homes, nobody will expect us to attend church this morning."

Papa then said Mr. Harmon was a man he could trust. He left to get Mr. Harmon to open the Z.C.M.I. store. When Papa returned he was carrying the beef jerky, hardtack, and four big water canteens wrapped in a flour sack.

121

I got Sweyn's saddlebags from the barn. Mamma filled them with beef jerky, hardtack, beans, and coffee. She also gave me an old coffeepot and frying pan, which Cal Roberts had forgotten. I carried them up to the loft. The outlaw looked everything over and was satisfied. Then I carried the canteens filled with water up to the loft. He made me take a swallow out of each canteen and then took a swallow from each himself. I guess he wanted to make sure we hadn't put salt or poison in the water.

"I'll just keep everything up here until mornin'," he said. "What is your ma fixin' for Sunday dinner?"

"Baked ham and sweet potatoes," I answered. "But she said to tell you that she'll fix anything you want."

"That'll do just fine for dinner," he said. "But tell her I want a big steak with fried potatoes and onions for supper."

I took Frankie and the outlaw their dinner at noon. I waited in the loft while they ate. Roberts sent me back to the kitchen for another piece of apple pie.

It was one of the few Sundays that Papa hadn't invited somebody for dinner. It was the only Sunday I could remember that we didn't have homemade ice cream for dessert.

I think that Sunday afternoon was the longest afternoon of my life. I was actually glad when the time came for me to do my chores, just to have something to do. Cal Roberts called down to me from the loft to give Dusty an extra feeding of oats. He also said he wanted a nose bag of oats to take with him.

We always had a cold supper on Sundays with leftovers from dinner. But Mamma decided to cook steaks for everybody because Cal Roberts wanted a steak. I took the outlaw and Frankie their supper.

When Roberts finished eating, he patted his stomach.

"A swallow or two of whiskey would go good right now," he said. "Ain't goin' to be able to get myself a drink for a spell. Your pa got any whiskey?"

"Yes, sir," I answered.

"Get me a bottle," he said. "And tell your pa I'm goin' to make sure the seal on it ain't broke. Don't want him thinkin' of puttin' knockout drops in it."

Papa only drank an occasional glass of brandy, but he always had whiskey in the house for company. I told him Cal Roberts wanted a bottle of whiskey and to make sure the government seal over the cork wasn't broken. Papa went to the pantry and got a quart bottle of whiskey. He handed it to me.

"Maybe he will get drunk and your uncle and I can surprise him," Papa said hopefully.

Cal Roberts proved himself too smart for that. When I gave him the quart of whiskey he looked at me and grinned.

"Now why would your pa give me a whole quart of whiskey?" he asked. "He could have given me a pint or even half a pint. Now watch closely, boy, so you can go back and tell your pa not to try to put anything over on Cal Roberts."

He opened the bottle. He took two big drinks from it. Then he held it over the side of the loft and poured the rest of the whiskey to the ground below.

Frankie was still tied up and watching. "The bad mans ain't going to let me go," he said, so solemnly that it shocked me.

"Of course he is," I said. "Papa and Mamma and Uncle Mark are going to do everything Mr. Roberts wants them to do. And Mr. Roberts has promised to leave you in the first town he passes through."

"He is going to leave me deaded," Frankie said.

123

The outlaw looked as astonished as I felt.

"What makes you say a thing like that?" I asked, thinking the outlaw had told Frankie he was going to kill him.

"I don't know how I know," Frankie said. "I just know he is going to leave me deaded."

Roberts leaned over and slapped Frankie very hard on the face. "You shut your trap, kid," he ordered.

I stared at the outlaw. "Why would he say a thing like that?" I asked.

"How should I know?" Roberts asked with a shrug. "I made a bargain with your pa and the Marshal. If they keep their end of the bargain, I'll keep mine. I'll drop the kid in the first town I come to after the twenty-four hours are up."

I said good night to Frankie and went back to the house. Papa was disapppointed when I told him what had happened to the whiskey. We ate supper in silence. After the dishes were done we all sat in the parlor. Mamma and Aunt Bertha had busy hands. They were always darning, sewing, crocheting, knitting, or doing something with their hands when they sat in the parlor after supper. But not this night. They both held their hands clasped tightly in their laps. Papa nervously smoked a cigar. I sat on the floor. Nobody talked until Uncle Mark came to the house.

"The men finished searching the ghost town," he said as he removed his Stetson hat and sat down.

"There will be no need for further pretense," Papa said. He got my notebook and handed it to Uncle Mark. "Here are a list of demands Roberts made J.D. write down. Tomorrow morning when he rides out of town with Frankie, everybody will know he has been in our barn. You've got to warn everybody in this town that every demand Roberts made is going to be met."

Uncle Mark read what I'd written in the notebook. "Now I know what was bothering me," he said as he finished. "Cal Roberts has no intention of leaving the boy alive."

"That is what Frankie told me!" I cried. "He said Roberts was going to leave him dead. He said it twice."

"I believe the boy has an eighteen-karat premonition," Uncle Mark said.

"What makes you arrive at that conclusion?" Papa asked.

"These demands," Uncle Mark said, tapping the notebook with his hand, "and a premonition of my own. Why does Cal Roberts want a week's supply of food? Why does he want four big canteens filled with water? Put them together and they only spell one thing. Roberts is going to head for Mexico. He will ride almost straight south from here, crossing the southwestern Utah desert to the Arizona line. Then he will cross the Arizona desert until he reaches Mexico."

"Even so," Papa said, "why should he kill Frankie?"

"He isn't going to slow down the mustang with the additional weight of the boy," Uncle Mark said. "And he isn't going to share precious water and food with him. He lied when he told John he would leave Frankie in some town. He has no intention of going anywhere near any town, knowing I might send telegrams to all the marshals between here and Mexico. The thousand dollars isn't going to satisfy a man like Cal Roberts. He wants his revenge in blood. He failed to kill the Judge, the District Attorney, and you. So he will kill Frankie instead, knowing all three of you would rather he had killed you than the boy. And believing he has a twenty-four-hour headstart, it is my guess he will kill Frankie within an hour after leaving town."

An agonized moan came from Mamma's lips. "Dear God in heaven, save my son!" she cried.

I added a prayer of my own as my entire body turned cold with fear.

"Cal Roberts must be killed before he leaves town," Uncle Mark said. Then he looked steadily at me. "You are positive, John, that he told you he was going to ride right down Main Street holding Frankie on the saddle with him?"

"Yes," I answered.

"His vanity may be his undoing," Uncle Mark said. "We will let him think we are meeting all his demands. I'll line Main Street with unarmed people all holding their hands over their heads. We will make him feel like a king as he rides down Main Street. He won't be expecting us to try and stop him."

"And just how do you propose to stop him without getting Frankie killed?" Papa asked.

"Hal Benson is the best sharpshooter in the county," Uncle Mark said. "I'll station Hal on the second floor of the Sheepmen's Hotel in a room with an open window facing Main Street. He will be armed with a Winchester repeater. Roberts will have his eyes on the crowd lining both sides of Main Street. When he passes the hotel, Hal Benson will shoot the gun out of his hand with the first shot. Then he will shoot to kill Roberts."

"No!" Papa exclaimed.

"I'd do it myself," Uncle Mark said, "but if Roberts doesn't see me standing unarmed with my hands over my head in the crowd, he will become suspicious."

"That isn't what I meant," Papa said. "The risk to Frankie is too great. Even if Hal succeeded in hitting the revolver in Roberts' hand, it could trigger the gun and kill Frankie. Roberts bragged about the hair trigger on his gun to J.D. And if, by a miracle, that didn't happen, the bullet from Hal's rifle could ricochet off Roberts' gun and kill Frankie. And if Hal missed the revolver with the first shot, Roberts would know the second shot would be aimed at his head and he'd kill Frankie."

"I grant the possibility of everything you have said," Uncle Mark admitted. "But I know if I let Roberts ride out of town with Frankie, I will be signing the boy's death warrant. I am going to convince you that my way is the only way if it takes me all night."

Mamma looked at the clock on the mantlepiece over the fireplace. "It is past your bedtime, John D.," she said.

I knew Mamma wasn't worried about me staying up late under the circumstances. She realized that Papa and Uncle Mark were going to end up in a real argument and didn't want me to hear.

I went up to my room. I sat on the edge of the bed without turning on the light. I had a terrible feeling that no matter who won the argument between Papa and Uncle Mark, Frankie would be killed. Uncle Mark had convinced me that Cal Roberts had no intention of leaving Frankie alive once they were out of town. Papa had convinced me that Uncle Mark was asking Mr. Benson to do the impossible. And there was Frankie's premonition of death. Why would a little four-year-old boy believe Cal Roberts was going to kill him? There was only one answer. It must be Frankie's guardian angel warning him of danger.

I got off my bed and knelt down. I clasped my hands in prayer.

"Dear God in heaven, please save Frankie," I prayed. "You must want him to live or you would have let him die with his family in Red Rock Canyon. Amen."

I got to my feet and reached for the beaded chain which

127

turned on the ceiling light. I pulled it sideways. The light came on. The beaded chain swung back and forth. I wondered why it kept swinging back and forth without stopping. Then a strange thing happened. The beaded chain began to dissolve and, plain as day, I saw Sweyn's lariat hanging from a rafter in our barn and my brother Tom climbing up it. Then once again all I could see was the chain and it had stopped swinging.

I remembered one time after an argument with Tom that I'd gone up to his loft and pulled the rope ladder up after me. When he hollered for me to throw it down, I leaned over the edge and gave him the good old raspberry. He had shouted that his great brain knew more than one way to get up to the loft. He'd taken Sweyn's lariat and thrown it over a rafter. Then he'd climbed up the lariat to the rafter and gone hand over hand across the other rafters until he reached the loft.

I'd told Uncle Mark that a man couldn't get to the loft without the rope ladder or bringing a wooden ladder into the barn. But a kid could. I didn't know exactly what I was going to do, but something told me to go to the barn. Maybe I could get to the loft without waking Cal Roberts, and grab his revolver and bowie knife and throw them over the edge.

I took the screen off the bedroom window and shinnied down the elm tree. Brownie barked softly and came running to meet me. I told him to be quiet and took him back to the doghouse, where Prince was sleeping.

"You stay," I said.

I knew Brownie wouldn't move until I gave him another command. I walked to the corral. It was a bright moonlit night without a cloud in the sky. I stood with my arms resting on the railing of the corral fence and stared at the barn. I knew if I tried to open the doors, the hinges would squeak and wake up the outlaw. Then I thought of the loose board at the rear of the barn which we often used as a shortcut or while playing hide-and seek. I walked softly to the rear of the barn. I lifted up the board. It squeaked, but very softly. A moment later I was in the barn.

I could see pretty well by the moonlight shining through the cracks on the sides of the barn. I looked up at the loft. I could see the cowboy boots of Cal Roberts sticking out over the edge of the loft. Tom had so much junk piled up in the loft and the outlaw was such a big man, I figured Roberts couldn't lie down without his ankles hanging over the edge. I could hear him snoring. I dropped my head and looked at Sweyn's lariat hanging from a wooden peg on the side of the barn.

Then another strange thing happened to me. Two words started repeating themselves in my mind: *Lariat, ankles. Lariat, ankles.* It was as if somebody was trying to tell me something. Oh how I wished I had a great brain like Tom. But I only had a little brain and it was up to me to figure it out. Just then Dusty moved in his stall, and suddenly I knew exactly what to do.

I walked softly to the livestock stalls. I let the horses smell me and patted them each on the nose. I scratched our milk cow behind the ears. Then I got the lariat. I held it coiled and walked to the center of the barn. And just as I'd seen Tom do it, I tossed the lariat upward letting it uncoil as it went. I wanted to drop half of it over the rafter. I missed the first time and the second time. But on the third try, half of the uncoiled lariat dropped over the rafter and uncoiled as it came down. I now had the lariat over the rafter.

I made a slipknot noose on one end of the lariat. I gave

129

myself plenty of slack as I placed the noose between my teeth. Then, using the double lariat, I climbed hand over hand up to the rafter. I grabbed it with both hands and let go of the lariat, except for the noose part between my teeth. Then I swung myself hand over hand from rafter to rafter until I came to the one closest to the loft. I pulled myself up and stood on the rafter.

I could see Cal Roberts lying on his back, a pillow under his head. He had a blanket over him except for his ankles. He was still snoring. Frankie was under a blanket in a corner with his back toward me. There was three feet separating me from the loft. This was going to be the hardest part. I placed the fingers of my right hand on the roof rafter between the sheathing and shingles and swung myself onto the loft. My feet touched just to the right of Roberts.

I removed the noose from my mouth. I was just stooping over to put it around the outlaw's ankles when his legs moved apart. I was afraid I'd awaken him if I tried to push his legs together. So I slipped the noose over just one ankle and tightened it carefully. I used the roof rafter to swing myself back to the crossbeam rafter. I hung from it with both hands and began to swing my body to give me momentum. Then I went hand over hand across the rafters until I was above the bales of hay. It was about a twenty-foot drop but seemed like a hundred before my feet landed on a bale of hay.

I climbed down and walked to where the other end of the lariat hung from the crossbeam rafter. I made a slipknot noose big enough to go over Dusty's head. Everything now depended upon the mustang. I walked to his stall. I patted him on the nose. I led him by the mane to where the lariat was hanging. I slipped the noose over his neck. I figured he could walk about thirty feet to the end of the barn.

"Please, God, make it work," I prayed.

Then I walked Dusty toward the end of the barn until the lariat began to tighten.

"Now Dusty!" I shouted, giving his mane a jerk.

Feeling the lariat tighten around his neck, the mustang seemed to know exactly what to do. He sprang forward. The lariat made a squealing sound as it slipped over the rafter. Dusty and I kept going. First the legs and then the body of Cal Roberts were dragged off the loft. Dusty and I took a few more steps and then stopped. Cal Roberts was upside down, swinging in a wide arc.

"What in the hell!" the outlaw shouted, startled, as he woke up.

His revolver had dropped from his holster as I thought it would when he was pulled off the loft. But the bowie knife was still in his scabbard. I saw him reaching for it. I knew he would try to lift himself up and cut the lariat.

"Stand, Dusty," I commanded the mustang.

I ran and grabbed a pitchfork. Roberts had the bowie knife out and was starting to lift himself up. I ran toward him and jabbed the pitchfork in his behind. He let out a yell and dropped the bowie knife. Then he reached for his revolver and found his holster empty. He began shouting the foulest oaths I've ever heard in my life. I ran and opened the barn door.

"Here, Brownie!" I shouted.

I had trained Brownie to go for help in case I was ever hurt. I lay down and grabbed my knee. When he came into the barn, I began groaning. He licked my face and then ran out of the barn, barking.

I was afraid to leave Cal Roberts alone because he might try to free himself. I was right. He had raised himself up. He

131

had hold of the lariat with one hand and was trying to loosen the noose around his ankle with the other hand. I grabbed the pitchfork and rammed it into his rump again. He let out a yell and let go of the lariat as he flopped upside down. But I wasn't taking any chances. I held the points of the pitchfork about two feet from his face.

"One move out of you and I'll ram this right into your face," I told him.

He didn't move but he called me every dirty name in the English language.

I heard footsteps running down the boardwalk in our backyard a couple of minutes later.

"In the barn!" I yelled.

I heard the corral gate open and then Mamma's voice.

"I told you that dog would never come scratching and barking at our front door unless John D. was in trouble," Mamma shouted.

"No trouble, Mamma!" I yelled. "I've got Cal Roberts hogtied!"

My shouting must have awakened Frankie. "John!" he shouted. "The bad mans is gone!"

Uncle Mark, Papa, Mamma, and Aunt Bertha came running into the barn. They stopped and stared at Cal Roberts hanging from the rafter upside down.

"Well, I'll be double-damned!" Uncle Mark said, and it was the first time I'd ever heard him swear.

"Please hurry, Uncle Mark," I said. "I need the lariat to get up to the loft to get Frankie."

My uncle removed a pair of handcuffs from his belt. "Just put your hands behind your back, Roberts," he ordered, "or I'll leave you hanging there until you do."

Cal Roberts put his hands behind his back. Uncle Mark

snapped the handcuffs on the outlaw's wrists. Then my uncle picked up the revolver and bowie knife.

"All right, John," he said. "Back up Dusty and let him down."

I grabbed Dusty's mane and backed him up until Roberts was lying on the ground. Uncle Mark removed the noose from his ankles and told him to stand up. He pointed the outlaw's revolver at his back.

"I'll lock him up in jail," Uncle Mark said, "and then I'm coming back. I want to hear how a nine-year-old boy captured the most dangerous outlaw and gunslinger I have ever known."

"Are you all right, son?" Papa asked, as Uncle Mark marched Cal Roberts off to jail.

"Papa!" Frankie shouted from the loft, as he recognized the voice.

"I'm just dandy," I said. "But Frankie is still tied up. Let me get him and then I'll tell you all about it."

I got up to the loft the same way I had before, with Mamma calling for me to be careful all the way. I untied Frankie and rubbed his wrists and hands. Then I made him grip my hands to prove the circulation was restored and he had the strength to hold on before I let him get on my back. I tossed the rope ladder over the edge of the loft and climbed down.

When we reached the ground, Papa, Mamma, and Aunt Bertha made a fuss over Frankie and then we all went into the house. While Mamma gave Frankie a bath and put him into a clean nightgown and robe, I told Papa and Aunt Bertha what had happened. Then Mamma came back into the parlor carrying Frankie in her arms. She sat down in her maple rocker, holding him in her lap. I had to tell Mamma about my capture of Cal Roberts. I had no sooner finished than Uncle Mark arrived, which meant I had to tell it for the third time. Then my uncle paid me a compliment that I didn't deserve.

"I don't believe," he said, speaking to Papa, "that Tom is your only son with a great brain."

"I know I haven't a great brain like Tom," I said. "But I'm satisfied with my own little brain. I prayed for a miracle and it happened when the swinging light chain gave me the idea of how to get up to the loft. Then I put my little brain to work and it worked just peachy dandy."

Papa looked at Frankie, who had gone to sleep on Mamma's lap with a contented smile on his face. "Mark had me about convinced his plan was the only possible way to save Frankie's life when Brownie came scratching and barking at the front door."

"I was right about Cal Roberts and the boy," Uncle Mark said. "Roberts knows he will be hung for killing those two prison guards. I asked him when I locked him up in jail what he had intended to do with Frankie. He said he had nothing to lose now by telling the truth. He intended to kill Frankie as soon as he was sure he wasn't being followed by a posse."

"Just what would Frankie's chances have been with your plan?" I asked.

"I didn't admit this to your father," Uncle Mark said, "but hitting a moving target as small as a revolver while shooting at a downward angle would have been about a hundred-to-one shot. But I figured one chance in a hundred to save the boy was better than no chance at all."

Uncle Mark got to his feet and walked over to me. "I'd better get going," he said. "But before I go, John, I want to

135

thank you. And the state of Utah is going to thank you also. There is a five-hundred-dollar reward for the capture of Cal Roberts."

I hadn't even thought about a reward. "I did it for Frankie, not for any reward," I said.

"You risked your life and earned the reward," Uncle Mark said. "There isn't a doubt in my mind that Cal Roberts would have killed you if he had woken up while you were in the loft or if his revolver hadn't fallen out of his holster."

I hadn't thought about the danger then and I couldn't think about it now. "Boy, oh, boy," I said. "Five hundred dollars makes Tom and his great brain look like a piker."

"It will go a long way toward paying for your education," Uncle Mark said.

"Education?" I asked. I felt my heart drop all the way down to the soles of my shoes.

"Wipe that disappointed look off your face, J.D.," Papa said, smiling. "Your mother and I have no intention of using the reward money for your education. We are paying to send your brothers to the Catholic Academy and we will pay to send you and Frankie when the time comes. But five hundred dollars is just too much money for a boy your age to have to spend. We will put the money in the bank and give it to you with the interest when you are eighteen."

What Papa said didn't quite wipe the disappointed look off my face. "Boy, oh, boy, that is a long time away," I said. "Can't I have any of it now?"

Mamma was rocking Frankie in her arms. "Why do you need more than your allowance now?" she asked.

"Well, for one thing," I said, "to buy new tires and a new sprocket for Tom's bike."

"That you can have," Papa said.

"And I figure I'm old enough to have a bike of my own," I said. "I want to buy a bike for me and a tricycle for Frankie."

"That you can also have," Papa said, smiling.

It just goes to prove what a fellow can get out of life by being himself. Me and my little brain, with God's help, had saved Frankie's life. Me and my little brain had put a dangerous outlaw and killer behind bars. Me and my little brain had made me the richest kid in Utah and got me a new bike. But best of all, me and my little brain had got me a younger brother who thought I was just about the greatest in the world.